DUMPED FOR VALENTINES

by

J. Sterling

DUMPED FOR VALENTINES

Edited by:

Jovana Shirley

Unforeseen Editing

www.unforeseenediting.com

Cover Design by:

Michelle Preast

www.Michelle-Preast.com

www.facebook.com/IndieBookCovers

Other Books by J. Sterling

Bitter Rivals – an enemies to lovers romance

Dear Heart, I Hate You

10 Years Later – A Second Chance Romance

In Dreams – a new adult college romance

Chance Encounters – a coming of age story

THE GAME SERIES

The Perfect Game – Book One

The Game Changer – Book Two

The Sweetest Game – Book Three

The Other Game (Dean Carter) – Book Four

THE PLAYBOY SERIAL

Avoiding the Playboy – Episode #1

Resisting the Playboy – Episode #2

Wanting the Playboy – Episode #3

THE CELEBRITY SERIES

Seeing Stars – Madison & Walker

Breaking Stars – Paige & Tatum

Losing Stars – Quinn & Ryson

THE FISHER BROTHERS SERIES

No Bad Days – a New Adult, Second Chance Romance

Guy Hater – an Emotional Love Story

VAL'S STEMS

"I HATE VALENTINE'S Day!" my floral assistant, Karina, yelled from the back room, and I giggled to myself before apologizing to the older woman standing in front of me.

"She's de-thorning the roses we got in this morning for the big day," I explained, and the woman simply grinned back.

"Those little pricks hurt like a bitch," she said with a wink before turning on her heel to leave with her order in hand.

I stood behind the counter with my jaw hanging open, shocked by the old woman's candor as I watched her walk out the door, the tiny bell jingling as it swung closed behind her.

"Did that old lady just say the word *bitch*?" Karina's

blonde head popped out from behind the wall, and I turned to cast a fake evil glare at her as she stepped into the room, standing next to me.

"You're one to talk. You can't shout obscenities from the back room, Karina! Everyone can hear you," I attempted to reprimand my best friend, but it was no use.

She was always shouting something or singing at the top of her lungs. I'd learned long ago that the girl had no volume control. And I loved her for it anyway.

Her head cocked back. "I didn't even use an *obscenity*, Valerie," she said, her tone mimicking mine before she continued, "I simply said that I hate Valentine's Day."

"And that's pretty much blasphemy in these parts, and you know it. Why don't you just take a shearing knife and stab me right in the heart?"

"Ooh, can I? Please?" she mocked, and I narrowed my eyes at her. "Then, I'd never have to take another thorn off these stupid life-sized roses again."

Karina had always loathed Valentine's Day, and she had no shame in letting everyone know it. Half the universe seemed to agree with her, calling it names and claiming it was a made-up, meant-nothing, thoughtless, stupid excuse to spend way too much unnecessary money, of a holiday.

I, on the other hand, was part of the group who loved it

and not just because I owned a floral shop. I thought Valentine's Day was sweet, romantic, and I didn't see why so many people complained about having an extra day to show their person just how much they loved them. Sure, it was a completely random date on a calendar that signified nothing of importance to most people, but why couldn't we go a little overboard for our significant other, or our children, or our best friends for no reason? See, I loved every single thing about it.

"Stop calling my roses stupid. They'll hear you."

"And probably murder me in my sleep," she bit back. "I bet they're plotting it now." She stabbed the air with her shears like she was fighting an invisible enemy.

For as much as Karina complained, I couldn't run the shop without her. She handled the books and the marketing and advertising, and she ran all of our social media accounts. She only had to get her hands dirty and help me with the flowers twice a year—Valentine's Day and Mother's Day. Since we'd opened, we were always overwhelmed with incoming and pending orders on both of those days. Even with a part-time staff of three, I needed the extra set of hands.

Karina pretended to hate it, but I knew it was only because she was single and mad that none of the roses were going to her. Which was why I'd had a dozen dropped off at her apartment earlier. I knew it wouldn't be the same, coming from me instead of a guy, but still, I wanted to brighten her otherwise empty apartment and make her smile.

"Stop taking your bitterness out on my sweet babies."

"Your sweet babies have torn up both my hands and almost every finger. They're evil." She held up her hands, and I laughed at the bandages wrapped around eight of her ten fingers. "You're laughing? You're actually laughing at my pain?"

Shaking my head, I informed her, "I'm just laughing because this happens every time. You never learn."

"It doesn't matter. It's not like I have anyone to keep my fingers pretty for. Unlike you. Where is Mr. Perfect taking you to dinner tonight?"

"Oblange," I said as a smile erupted.

"Ooh la la. The perfect place for the perfect proposal." She wagged her eyebrows at me.

I smacked her shoulder. "Stop it."

"No."

"You're not helping," I complained as my insides twisted at the thought.

"I'm not trying to help," she argued before cocking her

head to the side. "Wait, what am I not trying to help with?"

I laughed again. "You seriously just argued with me without thinking? You said the exact opposite thing for no reason other than to say it? Who are you?"

"Your best friend. Your business partner. Your future cat-owning roommate if neither one of us ever gets a ring put on it. Pick one."

I stood, smiling at my crazy best friend, wondering what on earth I'd do without her. The things that came out of her mouth never ceased to amaze or amuse me.

"Now, tell me why I wasn't helping. What's really going on?" All pretenses dropped, along with her trademark smile, as Karina grew serious and stepped toward me, putting one hand on my shoulder.

"I just don't want to get my hopes up," I admitted, but it fell on deaf ears. And on an even more deaf heart.

My hopes were already up. My heart was already hopeful. Proposing was the next step in my and Moore's relationship, and I'd be lying if I didn't think it was bound to happen any day now. Each time he asked me out to a fancy dinner, I donned a pretty dress and styled my hair and makeup perfectly just in case that night turned into *the night*. It might be a little vain, but I wanted to look nice for the pictures that I assumed would be taken without my knowing while he asked.

"It's been three years. If he doesn't ask you soon, I will." Her arm lowered, and she offered me an almost-sympathetic smile, which made me start to lose my composure.

We'd all met during college here in New York.

Karina and I had bonded in a junior year business class and had been inseparable ever since, coming up with a solid business plan for opening the flower shop together even though I was the majority owner. With or without Karina, Val's Stems was always going to be a reality, but we solidified the partnership one night over pizza and cheap boxed wine.

The two of us met Moore at a senior year mixer, where it seemed like everyone and everything gravitated around his pull. If the party were a match, then Moore was the oxygen the flame needed to survive. Take Moore out of the equation, and the whole thing snuffed out, faded to black, and died. I'd never been so taken with someone's energy before. He was so self-assured and confident. And after talking to him for a whole ten minutes, I was convinced I'd met someone who would change my life for the better.

Moore knew exactly what he wanted to do and what it would take to get there. Instead of the usual scared college senior who wasn't quite sure where they'd go after graduation, he seemed to have all his ducks in a row. I related to him on a visceral level. It had seemed like we were the only two people on campus who were tired of waiting to get degrees to start our real lives.

I sucked in a long breath, pulling it together. "He has been acting weird lately," I admitted, a little too excited for my own good.

"He's always weird. That's why you like him," Karina teased because weird was the very last thing Moore ever was.

"He's never weird," I countered.

Predictable, *stable*, and *motivated*—those words described him more accurately.

"You're right. He's probably just nervous because he's going to propose!" she shouted before disappearing into the back room at the same time the bell jangled with the opening of the door.

I tamped down my eagerness for tonight and turned to the approaching customer. "Hi there, sir. How can I help you today?"

ALL DOLLED UP

I HAD CHANGED three times before settling on the fitted red dress I wore underneath my long jacket. It was February in New York, and it was freezing. Still, I didn't want to dress for the weather in some oversize sweater and boots, not when tonight might possibly, maybe be *the night*. So, I'd dolled up for the potential occasion.

Ridding my mind of the wishful thinking, I walked through the solid wood doors of the restaurant and was immediately hit with warmth. Five steps inside, and I spotted Moore's perfectly coifed hair from the hostess stand and passed by without stopping to address her when she asked if I had reservations. I hadn't meant to be rude, but my excitement had gotten the best of me.

"Hey, Val." Moore rose from his seat, pulled me into a hug, and placed a chaste kiss on my cheek that felt more friendly than romantic.

Before I could overanalyze it, he pulled out my chair for me as I removed my jacket and folded it around my seat back.

"You look beautiful." He swallowed, and his voice sounded shaky.

Nerves, I assumed. Maybe tonight really was *the night*.

"Thank you," I said before getting comfortable at the latest hot spot in the city.

Honestly, the fancy dinners weren't my scene or style at all, but I knew they were Moore's, so I never argued or complained when he suggested eating at one.

A waiflike waitress appeared, a genuine smile on her face as she asked, "How are you two this evening?"

"Good, thank you," Moore responded for us both.

"Can I get you started with any wine or a drink from the bar?" She looked between us, giving us each equal amounts of attention.

I noticed these things because normally, women were taken with Moore, and they treated me as if I either wasn't there at all or like I was a nuisance, something to get out of the way.

"I think we're okay for now," Moore said before I could answer.

I really wanted a glass of merlot.

"I'll give you both some time with the menu," she said and disappeared as quickly as she had appeared.

Moore reached across the table, a silent signal that meant he wanted my hand in return. I placed my left hand in his, and he squeezed gently. "You know I care about you, don't you, Val?"

Care about me?

I nodded, my heart suddenly lodged firmly in my throat.

"But I don't think this is working anymore." He delivered the blow so softly, so nonchalantly, that I didn't realize his thumb had still been rubbing the side of my hand until I yanked it away abruptly.

"What isn't working anymore?" My mind refused to put the pieces together.

He flashed a smile. The same smile I was sure he donned at the office a thousand times in order to get whatever it was that he wanted. "Us, babe."

Babe?

Reality hit me with a swift kick to the guts. "Don't call me that," I stuttered as my vision instantly blurred.

"Sorry. Habit," he said as if that explained it away or made it okay.

"You're breaking up with me? Why? And why did you

bring me here if you were just going to dump me?" The questions burned my throat on their way out before the realization kicked me in the guts again.

He hadn't wanted me to make a scene, so he'd brought me to a public place—and an upscale one at that. The fact that he'd even thought I would create any semblance of a circus made me want to throw up. Did he even know me at all?

"We don't want the same things, Val. You have to see that."

"What do you mean? What things?" I asked because I was genuinely confused. Hadn't we always talked about living in the city and owning a place with a view of the park? Or had that always been my dream?

I suddenly found myself searching for conversations I wasn't even sure we'd ever had. I felt like I was living in a world of fiction, unable to separate reality from the words on the pages. Which version was the truth?

"I want to leave New York." His entire face lit up as he said those particular words.

I looked down at my glass of water, still completely full, before meeting Moore's brown eyes. "You want to leave? For how long? What about your job?"

"For a few years? Forever? I'm not sure." He shrugged

like he wasn't delivering relationship-changing news. "I don't ever want to stay in one place. I want to see new things and experience new cultures."

My body tightened in offense for New York, the city I'd known and loved my entire existence. Suddenly, this big, vibrant place with all of its life and culture wasn't good enough for him? There was always so much to do and see here. This city was teeming with energy, with a vibrancy that songs and books and movies were made about, were written for.

"We live in New York City. Why would you need to go anywhere else? There's more culture in ten blocks than in most places combined."

"See"—he leaned back, his shoulders relaxing—"that's exactly what I'm talking about. You're content with staying here forever and running your little flower shop on the corner."

He said the words as if what I'd accomplished since graduating meant nothing. He knew more than most people how hard I'd worked to secure loans and funding to get my business off the ground. I hadn't come from money and didn't have the perks that others had been born into. I had built the shop from nothing but hopes and dreams, and it thrived with my green thumb and love for it. And here he was, acting like what I had created was something small and insignificant … something anyone could do if they wanted.

"I am." I forced the words out. "I am content with that. The store is all I've ever wanted to do, and I'm doing it."

"Well, most people want more than that. They want to explore and have adventures. You consider riding the subway to the Bronx an adventure."

"Hey!" I all but shouted before lowering my voice. "Have you seen the people and all the different walks of life on that train? It *is* an adventure. Every borough in this state is an adventure. I'm sorry you can't see it."

"I see it. Just not the way you do."

"I'm happy where I am. And I thought you were too."

"I know you did. Look, Val, the truth is, I want to live in other countries for months on end before going to another one and starting all over."

"You do?" My voice caught on the air around me, which had grown thick since our conversation had started. How come we'd never talked about this before? Why was it only coming to light now? Since when had I started dating a gypsy?

"I do."

"Since when?"

"Since my firm offered me a position in London for a

year."

"London?" I squeaked out. "A year?"

"Yeah. Doesn't it sound great? I've always wanted to go. And a year! Can you imagine?" He was so excited that it was like I wasn't even in the room, much less the equation. And I guessed, to be honest, I really wasn't.

"It sounds like a great opportunity for you." I tried not to sound as bitter as I currently felt, but it was a struggle. I'd thought I'd end the night as Moore's fiancée, not his ex-girlfriend. How could I have been so wrong?

"I didn't ask you to come with me to London because I knew you'd say no."

All the air left my lungs with his words. He wasn't wrong, but why did him being right make me feel so small? Even if I had said no, he still should have asked, at least given me the opportunity to choose. Instead, he'd made the choice for me.

"You didn't even ask though."

"I didn't want to put you in the position of choosing between me or the shop."

My jaw tensed as my anger started to elevate. "Don't do that."

"Do what?"

"Pretend like you were sparing my feelings."

His lips pursed together before he asked, "Would you have said yes?"

I shook my head, confirming his gut instincts. "I love it here. This is my home. I opened my shop in this city for a reason. I can't up and move and leave it all behind."

"You could," he countered.

"But I don't want to," I stated firmly.

"I know." His tone sounded almost sympathetic, and I had to stop the tears from falling.

I was frustrated, angry, and hurt.

"I haven't changed," I said, wondering if I'd misled him the past three years somehow. Had I said something that could have made him think I wanted to leave New York eventually and live somewhere else? I was certain I hadn't. The thought had never crossed my mind, so there was no way it'd ever crossed my lips.

"I know that too. But I have. I want more. I want to do so many things. And you don't have an adventurous bone in your body."

"Can you stop offending me, please?" I managed to get out before the first tear fell.

"I'm sorry. You're right. I didn't mean for it to go this way exactly."

"What did you expect?" I asked as more tears fell. There

was no stopping them now.

He blew out a harsh breath before pulling his jacket over his arms. "I … I don't know. I'll send your things over to the store. You can just get rid of whatever I have at your place. I won't have room for it anyway."

His words washed over me before I finally pieced it all together. "You're already leaving, aren't you? That's why you've been so weird, so distant lately? You already accepted the position, right?"

He stared at me, his jacket now firmly fastened across his body.

He still hadn't answered my question, so I asked it again in a different way. "When do you leave, Moore?"

"The day after tomorrow," he answered, confirming my suspicions before pushing away from the table and taking two steps toward me. I didn't move or look up as he planted a kiss on the top of my head. "I sort of feel like a real asshole right now, but this is for the best. You'll see that eventually."

I said nothing as he walked away and left me sitting there, alone, with my aching heart and beat-up pride.

Three years wasted. Three years spent with someone I'd thought I knew inside and out, whom I apparently hadn't known at all.

Gathering up my coat, I stood tall as I walked out of the swanky restaurant I swore I'd never step foot in again. No more eating in places where the dessert cost more than a dozen of my finest roses.

Instead of hailing a cab, I decided to walk home. I craved the cold air to clear my head. Before I knew it, I'd be home, calling Karina to fill her in, and I needed the solitude and quiet that the walk provided. Not that New York was ever quiet by any means, but sometimes, it seemed softer than Karina could be.

I walked alone, just me and my thoughts. And Moore's words echoing in my head like a broken record.

Not adventurous. I guffawed to myself.

Why would I leave New York? I continued my conversation with the night sky. *Who wants to? Only an idiot wants to leave this city.*

"And that's fine because I don't date idiots, and I definitely don't marry them," I shouted to whoever might be listening, no doubt sounding like a crazy person to anyone watching.

Yet all the while, in the back of my mind, I wondered if Moore was right. I'd barely scratched the surface in terms of traveling. I hadn't even seen much of my own country, let alone any others.

"Not adventurous," I repeated out loud again as I rounded the corner of my condo building.

I could be adventurous.

I could be anything I damn well wanted.

I'd show him.

LAST-MINUTE VACATION

I STRUGGLED TO unlock the door to the shop, balancing the two coffees I held in my hands and praying they wouldn't spill. Heaven forbid I actually placed one of them on the ground to make this easier on myself. Turning the key enough to hear it unlatch, I bumped the door with my hip, and it swung wide open, the little bell jingling in its wake. Placing the still-full coffees on the counter, I smiled to my-self at the small victory. Not a single drop wasted.

Reaching for my apron, I tied it around my waist and surveyed the room. The windows were painted with red and white hearts and Cupid shooting his arrow. Words like *Be Mine* and *I'm Yours* greeted potential customers in a swirly script-like font. Even my newly single status couldn't dampen my love for this holiday. It still made me smile.

All night, I'd tossed and turned—after I finally stopped

crying. At some point through my tears, I'd realized that I wasn't as brokenhearted as I should have been about losing Moore. I was sad and hurt, for sure, grieving more the loss of what felt like wasted time, but I wasn't necessarily destroyed by the split. After three years, shouldn't I have been more devastated?

Maybe Moore had known what he was talking about when it came to us. He had clearly seen something that I hadn't. Or maybe with my attention focused so singularly on my business and its growth, I couldn't see what was right in front of me. I'd convinced myself that us seeing each other only a couple nights a week was normal for two hard-working people. It was easy to make excuses for other things in your life when you ran your own business and felt solely responsible for its success.

The bell jangled, and I turned in time to see Karina walk in, a giant smile on her face. I hadn't called her last night. I hadn't called anyone.

"Ooh, is this for me?" She reached for one of the coffee cups before taking a swig.

"Well, it is now," I said playfully, moving my own coffee out of her reach.

"So," she started before she all but burst at the proverbial seams, "let me see it!"

"See what?"

"The ring, dummy." She reached for my left hand and came up empty. She searched my right hand—the wrong one—before dropping it to my side. "No proposal? Again? Ugh!"

My eyes instantly filled with tears at the thought of saying what had happened out loud. "Not exactly," I said before wiping at my face and willing the tears to disappear. In this moment, I felt more embarrassed than anything else.

"Oh my gosh. Val, what happened?"

"He broke up with me."

She leaned back against the refrigerated glass case. "He what?" she asked, her tone incredulous.

"He took a job in London. Said he wants to travel the world and I don't ever want to leave New York, so ..." I trailed off as my email dinged out a notification.

"He took a job in London without talking to you first?" She reached for her coffee and took a tentative sip. "Asshole."

I shrugged. "He said I had no sense of adventure. That I didn't want to go anywhere or do anything outside of the five boroughs."

"What's wrong with the five boroughs?" she asked gruffly.

"That's exactly what I said." I shifted my weight and clicked on the most recent email on my laptop.

The subject line screamed, *Last-Minute Deal to Vail! 5-star resort, just in time for Valentine's!* In my emotion-filled night, I'd completely forgotten that I'd signed up for at least half a dozen travel sites, hoping that one of them might give me the ammunition I needed to prove Moore wrong.

Karina peered over my shoulder. "What is that? Vail? Like, in Colorado? I've always wanted to see Colorado," she said wistfully.

"Really?" I asked, realizing that I'd never truly longed to go anywhere other than where I was. Maybe I wasn't so normal after all.

"Yeah. It looks so pretty with all the trees and those big ole mountains. Don't you think?"

I shrugged. "I guess." I clicked the link, and gorgeous pictures filled my screen. "Wow," I said without thinking.

"That's what Vail looks like?" Karina asked, knowing full well I had no idea. "It's adorable!"

"It's stunning." I continued to scroll through the pictures of the resort, feeling like I was looking at some sort of winter wonderland I'd never experienced before. The decor and style weren't like anything we had in New York, and I found myself almost shocked by it.

"You have to go." She clapped her hands together like the most brilliant idea on the planet had entered her brain.

"I can't just"—I paused—"go."

"Why not?"

I clicked on the button to get more information. As I scanned the fine print, I sighed. "Because the deal is only for this coming weekend."

"So?"

"So, it's almost our busiest day of the year, for one," I started before she stopped me cold.

"First of all, we both know that our busiest day of the year is Mother's Day. And your precious favorite holiday isn't until next Thursday." She peered over my shoulder again. "According to this, you'll be back by Monday."

"But I'd be gone for three full days. Right before—"

She cut me off again, not wanting to hear my excuses, "I can handle things here. I've been working by your side for years. I know more than you think. And the kids will be here, too, so I won't be alone."

The "kids" were the three part-time employees I'd hired over a year ago. They were young, but they were dependable, and they loved working at the shop, so I knew we could count on them to pull their weight.

Looking back at my screen, I felt a slight tug in my guts. That little pull that people talked about when they saw a place that called to them, I was feeling it.

"It looks so magical," I all but whispered, and Karina agreed.

"You should go. Really, Val. I wish you could see your face right now," she said, and the smile I hadn't known I was wearing instantly grew in size. "Do something nice for yourself since that dickhead dumped you right before your favorite holiday."

I bristled, my eyes squeezing shut for only a moment before reopening. "He wasn't a dickhead."

Why was I defending him?

He was totally a dickhead.

"He had a last name for a first name."

"What does that have to do with anything?"

"Just another reason for me to hate him and think he's dumb. Let me trash him however I see fit."

Genuinely smiling for what felt like the first time since last night, I agreed. "It was a stupid name. Who names their kid Moore anyway?"

"That's the spirit. Now, book that damn trip before I book it for you." She hopped up on top of the floral counter and crossed her legs, still sipping on her coffee when I hadn't even touched mine.

Could I really leave?

"Don't second-guess yourself, Val. I know you. You haven't taken more than one day off since we opened the store. You deserve this. And maybe some hot Colorado guy to go with it."

I laughed at the notion before sucking in a breath. I was immediately hit with a realization that shouldn't have surprised me at all but still managed to. I actually *wanted* to go. I wanted to get away from New York even if it was only for a few days. It wasn't something I'd ever considered before last night, but now, snow-covered mountains and old-world charm seemed to call to me. How could something so foreign imprint itself inside me so quickly?

"I don't hear the click of the keyboard." Karina waved a hand in front of my face.

I snapped out of my Vail-induced daze. "I'm going to do it," I announced.

A grin a mile wide spread out over her cheeks. "Good. I was worried for a second."

Confusion filled me as I asked, "That I wouldn't go?"

"No. That you might let Moore ruin this day for you. Or worse, that you might start hating love."

A hearty laugh roared from my chest. "Never going to

happen. I'm not the cynical one. And I *love* love too much to ever give up on it."

"Thank goodness because you do own a damn flower shop, you know." She finished off her coffee and slammed the empty cup on the counter with a loud slap. "Book that trip before you come to your senses!" She hopped down and made her way toward the back stockroom. "I'm going to spend time with the murderers. Wish my fingers luck."

"You could wear gloves, you know," I shouted back.

"I don't hear any clicking!"

COLORADO

WALKED OFF the plane, thankful to be on solid ground after the turbulence that had greeted me midair and made me pray for my life on more than one occasion. Thin mountain air was no joke, and the three women who had thrown up in their paper bags behind me were proof of that.

After retrieving my luggage in the smallest airport I'd ever laid eyes on, I headed outside, where a car was waiting to drive me to the resort. It was included in the last-minute deal I'd booked after Karina threatened to book it for herself if I didn't. Jealousy had torn through me at the challenge.

I fired off a quick text, letting her know I'd made it to Colorado alive, no thanks to the giant metal object that had cut through the air like a roller coaster with no track. Settling into the backseat of an SUV, I made small talk with the driver. Karina's response came almost instantly, where she informed me that the shop was in good hands and to please enjoy myself.

Another text immediately followed.

I HOPE YOU DO SOMETHING ADVENTUROUS THIS WEEKEND ... AND I DON'T MEAN SNOWBOARD, IF YOU CATCH MY DRIFT.

I shook my head as another text appeared.

AND IF YOU DON'T CATCH MY DRIFT ... I MEAN, HAVE AN ADVENTURE WITH A MAN. A HOT ONE. ONE YOU'LL NEVER HAVE TO SEE AGAIN. I HOPE YOU ADVENTURE ALL OVER VAIL WITH HIM, STARTING IN A HOT TUB. THEN, MAYBE OUTSIDE IN THE SNOW. WE'LL CALL IT A MANVENTURE. I HOPE YOU MANVENTURE YOUR STUPID EX RIGHT OUT OF YOUR SYSTEM. MANVENTURE ALL OVER THE PLACE. AND SEND ME UPDATES!

I clicked the button on my phone that made her ridiculous text disappear before realizing that I was actually a little excited. I'd convinced myself on the flights over that I would have fun, let loose, and genuinely give in to whatever Vail decided to bring me. When I'd originally packed, I was worried that I wouldn't be able to detach enough from the store to actually have a good time, and the last thing I wanted was to be in this beautiful place and not have the gumption to enjoy it.

"We're almost there, Miss Hamilton," the driver announced from the front seat, and I thought how quick that had been.

I redirected my attention from the phone screen to my surroundings and felt my heart pang inside my chest. The tree-lined roads were snow-covered and looked like something straight out of a holiday movie.

The SUV pulled to a stop in front of the resort that looked exactly the way it had online, and I breathed out in relief. I hadn't truly questioned the deal before I booked it, but now that I had arrived, I realized that things weren't always as nice as they advertised. This resort was the exception to the rule.

"It's beautiful, isn't it?" the driver asked as he pulled my suitcase from the back.

"It really is. I feel like I've stepped into another world," I said, my voice sounding breathier than I'd intended.

"Everything here is inspired by Europe," he added with a smile. "I hope you have a great time."

"Thank you," I said before handing him a cash tip.

Turning around to face the main building, I took in the view before I even thought about moving even though it was freezing out here. It felt much colder here than it had back in New York. Retail shops filled the lower levels of each building for as far as I could see, and hordes of people milled about what basically looked like a quaint town square.

Valentine's Day themes painted on clear glass reminded me of my own storefront back home, and my heart panged for only a second before settling. I smiled to myself at the idea that no matter where you traveled, businesses seemed to celebrate in similar ways. Each one wanted to entice the potential buyer. They made whatever they sold relevant to not only the holiday, but also to your life in an attempt to convince you that you couldn't live without what they had to offer.

My eyes skirted past the stores and landed on an oval-shaped ice-skating rink that was filled to the gills with skaters and people-watchers. Couples held hands as they tried to stay upright on the ice. Looking away from the rink, I focused on all of my non-human surroundings. There was a lot to take in. Eye-catching architecture with so much detail seemed to be everywhere I looked.

A large, ornate clock tower was in the distance, and it dinged as soon as I looked at it, as if telling me hello. The buildings, with their delicate paint jobs and Swiss chalet–inspired balconies, made me feel like I was in one of my mom's old music boxes come to life. Vail was romantic, elegant, and like I'd originally thought back in New York when I was only seeing it on my computer screen—*magical*.

As I inhaled a long, cold breath, excitement filled my lungs, and I decided to finally go inside the hotel. Making my way through the main lobby area to check in, I noticed that there were a few people in line ahead of me. Instead of reaching for my phone like I normally would have, I watched them instead. Vail seemed to be a haven for couples in love, and I momentarily felt my heart hitch inside my chest. I wondered if I'd made a mistake, coming here at this time of year. Would my breakup be thrown in my face the whole time? Would I be sad instead of adventurous? The last thing I wanted was to spend my time here wallowing in self-pity and replaying old conversations between Moore and me, wondering where it had all gone wrong.

But when the couple in front of me couldn't keep their hands or their lips off each other, I recognized what the feeling inside of me was. It was joy. Instead of being filled with bitterness at their public declarations, I was happy for them. They smiled and kissed each other no less than seven times in what seemed like thirty seconds, almost as if their very lives had depended on breathing in the other's air.

Moore and I had never been that affectionate, not in public or in private. He never needed my air. And I realized, too, that I had never needed his. I breathed just fine on my own.

My heart surprised me as it thumped out, not with sadness for what I'd recently lost, but with hope for what was to come. I wanted to find a love like that someday. I wanted to be with someone who needed my air to breathe.

That kind of passion.

Moore and I hadn't had it for each other, but we had it for our respective jobs. It wasn't enough to just have one and not the other. I craved them both. And right now, in this moment, I knew it was possible. My heart was literally telling me with each beat.

In front of my lovesick duo stood a dark-haired guy holding a notebook and a fancy digital camera in his hands. He was balancing what looked like a heavy bag on his shoulder. I could tell from the way his muscular body tilted to one side, his back heaving with each breath he took, that it must have weighed a lot. I wondered if he was here alone like I was or if some gorgeous female would appear at his side at any second. He turned to face me, his striking blue eyes looking right into mine, causing my heart to stop for a second.

WHOA, my heart said.

Did I ask the question out loud?

I knew I hadn't.

At least, I didn't think that I had.

Mr. Blue Eyes smiled, and I noticed a pair of dimples on his cheeks before he turned away and walked toward the woman at the check-in counter calling for him. My eyes followed his movements as he sauntered, catching on the broadness of his shoulders before moving down to his hips and his ass. I was definitely enjoying the view, and I'd be damned if he didn't turn around at that moment and catch me staring. I wanted to look away, but it was too late.

Fanning my cheeks with my embarrassment, I continued waiting in the queue for my turn, still reeling from being caught. As luck would have it, I ended up right next to my handsome stranger, who I tried my hardest not to ogle at even though everything in me wanted to memorize that body. If I'd thought he was attractive at a distance, he was even sexier up close. Too sexy for his own good.

And mine. The thought flitted into my mind before flitting back out.

Maybe I would take Karina's advice and have a *man-venture* this weekend. What harm could it cause?

MANVENTURE FOR ONE

W ITH MY KEY card in hand, I made my way to the third floor. Flinging open the ornate door, I stopped in the entryway for a second to take it all in. The view that greeted me was stunning, the colors of the room in deep reds and golds. Snow-covered mountains could be seen out the floor-to-ceiling windows, and a stone fireplace, just begging to be lit, called my name in the corner.

The plush king bed had thick drapes hanging behind it and over the top half, reminding me of something straight out of a princess storybook. As a matter of fact, the entire room looked like what I assumed a European castle must have looked like back in the day. Or maybe they still did? I honestly had no idea.

Part of me wanted to snuggle in that oversize bed with a good book, but the rest of me knew it didn't make any sense to spend my entire time here, being antisocial and avoiding all human contact. With a determined look on my face and a mission in mind, I tossed my suitcase onto the bed and pulled out my makeup bag. Freshening up a little, I decided not to change my clothes, and I headed down to the hotel bar.

The bar was located in the main restaurant, and I almost lost my nerve, turning right back around and stepping back into the elevator, when the hostess stopped me.

"Are you looking for someone?"

"Oh, no. I just wanted to go to the bar. Is that allowed?"

She smiled sweetly at me, her customer service top-notch. "Of course it is. Head straight through this hallway and toward the back. You can't miss it."

"Thank you." I smiled back, forcing the nerves in my belly to settle.

"And by the way," she whispered, "it turns into a total hot spot in about an hour." She glanced at her watch before giving me another grin. "Lots of hot, single men."

"Thanks for the tip." I maneuvered through the rose-covered tables and the air filled with so much romance that you could almost choke on it.

I reached the actual bar and breathed out a small sigh of relief when I spotted one single chair available. Rushing toward it before anyone else could beat me, I pulled the heavy stool back before sitting down in it and attempting to wiggle it forward. It was way too heavy and refused to budge.

"Miss Hamilton, let me help," a strange voice offered.

I turned to my right to see none other than the gorgeous, dark-haired, blue-eyed stranger from earlier. I almost fell face-first out of my seat when I saw him up close.

He stood up, reached for my stool, and inched it closer to the bar without any effort.

"How did you know—" I started to ask how he knew my last name before he jumped in and interrupted.

"I heard the woman say your name at the check-in counter." He extended his hand toward me. An introduction of sorts even though he hadn't told me his name yet.

I noticed he hadn't changed out of his earlier clothes either, and for whatever reason, that made me feel better about choosing to stay in mine.

"I'm Jase Malone. And that was kind of creepy, huh?"

I giggled but took his hand anyway as he gave me a firm shake. "A little, but would it be creepier if I told you I didn't mind?" I flirted without even thinking. It'd spilled out so easily. I thought it was because this guy was handsome as hell and I liked what I saw.

"I think I've lost credibility on what's considered creepy or not," he said with a small laugh as he signaled the bartender our way. "Can I buy you a drink, Miss Hamilton?"

When was the last time someone bought me a drink? I thought to myself.

That kind of thing happened in books and movies, but it wasn't something that had ever happened to me in real life before. Moore buying me drinks hadn't counted.

"Sure." I perused the menu that he'd handed me. "And it's Val."

"Short for ..." He trailed off, waiting for me to answer his unasked question.

"Valerie. But no one calls me that."

"All right, Val, not Valerie. Do you know what you'd like to drink?"

I looked at his glass, curious as I noted the stick of cinnamon poking out from behind a sprig of grass or something green. "What are you drinking?"

"I honestly don't remember what it's called, but it's one of their whiskey concoctions." He held the glass in the air.

"Is it good?"

"Surprisingly so."

He moved his glass toward my face, and I bent down to give it a good sniff. Usually, I hated the smell of whiskey, but his drink looked so amazing that I thought it might change my mind. Nope. It still smelled like death. Hard pass from me.

"Okay. Definitely not that," I said with a laugh as I continued to read the menu, which was broken down by type of spirit. That was actually helpful. After settling on gin, I picked my poison.

"Ready?" he asked, and I nodded, the bartender suddenly reappearing like an apparition.

"I'll take the Fred and Ginger," I said with a confident smile. God, I really hoped this drink was good.

Jase settled into his seat, propping one arm around the back of it as his fingertips grazed the side of my arm. "So, Val, what brings you to Vail?"

Pressing my body against the hard wood of the stool, I exhaled, "Do you want the CliffsNotes or the long version?"

He glanced up at the ceiling, his lips pursing together as he tapped them with one finger, as if deep in thought. His finger moved from his mouth to the air as his eyes clashed with mine. "I'll take CliffsNotes for two hundred, Alex."

He referenced *Jeopardy!*, and I stopped myself from calling his bluff because there was no way in hell this gorgeous specimen of a man sat around, watching that particular show for fun on weeknights. It was a pretty judgmental thought, I knew, but still.

"CliffsNotes it is. I got dumped by my boyfriend of three years on the night I thought he might propose. He's moving to London. He said I didn't have an adventurous bone in my body," I offered with a shrug as my cocktail appeared in front of me, almost too pretty to drink. "And now, I'm here."

"To prove him wrong?" he asked, his tone strictly curious, like he was trying to figure me out.

"I think it was about that at first, but I'm not so sure anymore." Dried grapefruit and lemongrass decorated the top of an old tin cup, and I immediately pulled out my phone and opened the camera app. "I know this is super annoying, but this is the prettiest drink I've ever seen. I have to take a picture of it."

Jase smiled. "I did the same thing with mine before you got here."

I swatted his arm like we were old friends. "You did not!"

He reached for his phone and pulled up his photo gallery, showing me the three pictures he'd taken of his own concoction.

"You really did." I knew I sounded shocked, but his blunt honesty was refreshing. And charming. "And, hey, those pictures are really good."

"Thanks," he said with a slight grin before tucking his phone back into his pocket.

I liked that he didn't have it sitting on the bar between us, where it could interrupt us or divert his attention.

"So, why are you here?" I asked as I sipped my cocktail. It was as refreshing as it was delicious. I wanted a hundred more of them.

"I'm a writer."

"Hence the notebook?" I pointed at the three-ringed binder I'd seen him with earlier, which still sat firmly in place at the top of the bar in front of him.

"Exactly."

My curiosity was piqued, my interest elevated. "What do you write? Books?"

"No. I'm a writer for a travel magazine and their online blog. I'm here to write a story about the resort and the romance of Vail," he said in a fake accent, rolling his eyes.

"Why the eye-rolling? Do you not normally write romance blogs?" I asked seriously because I had no idea how that all worked. Ask me about flowers, arrangements, and all things floral, but I knew very little about anything else.

He choked on the ice from his drink. "No. Definitely not. My colleague got injured and couldn't make this trip.

Forty-eight hours ago, I had no idea I'd be here."

You and me both, buddy, I almost said.

"Was your girlfriend upset that you came without her?" I looked away, pretending that I hadn't just baited that hook specifically so I could find out if he was single or not.

"I don't have a girlfriend," he said with a sexy smirk. "Or a wife before you fish for that one next."

A sound escaped my lips at him not only catching me, but also calling me out. I was thankful that he was single. I angled my body toward him as I finished off my drink and asked for another. I didn't expect Jase to pay for my drinks, as I could afford them on my own, but I'd deal with the bill later.

"So, what do you normally write about then, if it's not romance and resorts?"

His jaw stayed set, his blue eyes wild, as if he was considering how exactly to answer me. "It would be easier if I showed you."

The bartender placed another Fred and Ginger in front of me, and I went to work, slushing the ice into the mixture with my straw. "Okay?" I wasn't sure what that meant exactly, and I feared he was about to pull out his last twenty articles and force me to read them right here at this bar. I would do it, but it would be awkward.

"Come with me tomorrow, and I'll show you what I normally do. Plus, I'll need the help for the romance stuff, and I'm sure you're better at it since you're a girl and all."

"Oh jeez. Thanks for noticing."

"I'd have to be blind to not notice you," he said.

I felt my cheeks flush. Receiving compliments was always a little uncomfortable, to be honest, but I still liked getting them. And I definitely liked hearing it come from his lips. Those super-kissable, *Lord help me* lips.

"You'll come?" The smile he gave me lit up the whole bar, and I wondered how any woman refused Jase when he asked for something.

"Does anyone ever tell you no?" I teased, the alcohol already making my head spin. I felt looser, more relaxed, and willing to play. The drink allowed me to forget that I hadn't been single in three years and really had no clue what the hell I was doing or even if I was doing it right or well.

"Come on, Val," he said as he moved his hand to my arm. "No one can resist these." He smiled and pointed a finger at his dimples, and I had to agree. Those dimples were panty-droppers. Killer of lady bits. Ovary-exploders. Part of his, *I think I just got pregnant from that* look.

And it wasn't as if I had any other plans anyway. I hadn't even looked into things to do at Vail before I came here. I had been too busy making sure the store would continue running and not fall apart in my absence. I offered him a quick shrug before taking a gulp of my gin deliciousness.

"Are you stalling?" he pushed.

"No," I lied.

"Come with me. I promise you won't regret it."

I already knew that much. "Okay," I agreed. "I'll go with you."

"See? You're more adventurous already. Your ex-boyfriend was an idiot."

I laughed out loud. It might have been the second drink, but I couldn't have cared less. I felt really good, being here with him. I belonged in this bar, flirting with this sexy man. And Moore could go straight to hell for all I cared.

"So, where are you from?"

It was such an innocent question but one I wasn't sure I wanted to answer. Yes, I was having a nice time, getting to know Jase, and I planned on spending tomorrow with him, but did I want him to know where I lived and worked? It all felt a little too personal, a little too quickly, even though he'd told me that he was a travel writer for a magazine. It was too late to try to play the elusive *let's not tell each other anything personal* game.

I must have hesitated for too long because Jase laughed

like I sincerely amused him. "Too soon?"

"I haven't decided yet," I answered honestly before feeling a little stupid for being apprehensive.

I'd already told this guy about Moore. Of course he was eventually going to ask where I was from. Which would lead to him asking where I worked and I'd have to tell him that I owned a little flower shop that held my heart.

A groan escaped as I leaned my head back, closed my eyes, and answered like he'd pulled the information from the depths of my soul against my will, "New York. I'm from New York," I admitted, opening my eyes to see his expression.

A devilish grin appeared, coupled with those damn baby-making dimples. "No way."

I narrowed my gaze at him. "What?"

"Me too." That smile stayed firmly planted on his lips as he asked, "What part?"

"I live in the city. You?"

Everyone from New York knew that when you referenced *the city*, you were talking about Manhattan.

"I live in the city." He finished off his whiskey drink before asking for a straight shot of bourbon, neat.

What were the odds that I'd come on this last-minute trip and met someone who not only lived in the same state as I did, but also the same part of said state? This seemed a little too coincidental, almost like something I'd catch on a Hallmark movie. Not that I had a lot of time to watch those, but when I did, I binged.

"And you travel a lot?" I asked, feeling like my recent conversation with Moore was being tossed in my face again somehow. Another hot guy who loved to see the world and wanted to leave the rest behind.

"More than I'd like to, to be honest. I don't see the need to leave New York," he said with such confidence that it made my jaw drop. His eyes fell to my mouth. "What'd I say wrong?" he asked, attempting to backtrack his statement. "I just meant that—" He stopped short as I cut him off by waving my hand in the air.

"Nothing. I just really, really agree. And I was starting to think I was crazy for feeling like that."

"New York has everything in one place. People don't even realize," he started to explain, as if he needed to convince me. He had no idea he was preaching to the proverbial choir here.

"I know!"

"I usually write about the things and places that other people aren't talking about. I like to bring attention to places that make a real difference for either the owner or the community."

If I'd thought my curiosity was piqued before, it was tenfold now. And if I'd thought I was attracted to Jase Malone five minutes ago, it was nothing compared to the desire currently running through my body.

"Like what?"

"Tomorrow, Val, all your questions will be answered. Promise."

My body heated up and tingled. It wasn't the alcohol anymore. It was him.

"Then, I should probably go back to my room and rest?" I said it like a question because I was afraid if I didn't leave soon, I might end up drinking so much that he would have to carry me up to my room.

We all knew what would happen next: I'd beg him to stay. He'd say no at first—because he was a gentleman, of course—but I wouldn't take no for an answer. We'd have sex that would be so deliciously mind-blowing, but I'd forget all about it in the morning. Not because my mind had been blown, but because alcohol had made me forgetful. And forgetting something like that would be a crime to women everywhere.

And I was not about to sleep with this man and then *forget about it*!

That was absolutely unacceptable. If I had a manventure with Jase this weekend, I planned on remembering every single sordid detail, so I could replay it over and over again whenever I needed the inspiration.

"I'll meet you in the lobby at eight thirty," he said. There was no discussion or disagreeing.

"Eight thirty," I said with an approving nod.

"Don't eat first," he commanded.

I pulled a twenty from my purse and set it on top of the bar. "For my drinks," I mentioned before he started to complain, shoving it back in my direction. "Or give it to him as an extra tip." I nodded toward the bartender at the other end of the room.

Jase exhaled and looked slightly defeated. He didn't like me paying for things, and I'd be damned if that didn't turn me on even more. "Tomorrow, Val."

"Tomorrow, Jase. Good night." I turned on my heel and walked away, feeling his stare on my back. A woman knew when she was being watched, and I made sure to add a sway in my hips to give him a little something extra to look at.

You want to watch me walk away, Jase? I'll give you something to see.

Being on vacation mode brought out a new kind of boldness in me I'd thought I only saved for the store. Taking risks for my business seemed easy for me. I'd do whatever it took to make sure my flower shop not only survived, but also thrived.

Taking risks with my heart and my body was always the more difficult decision. I'd always played it safe. Not to mention the fact that it had been years since I'd been single, but Jase Malone seemed worth the risk. Even if it was only just for the weekend, I'd have one hell of a story to keep me warm on those cold winter nights back home.

JASE FREAKING MALONE

S WIPING ONE LAST coat of mascara on my eyelashes, I checked my reflection in the gold-trimmed bathroom mirror. The water here had made my usually thick, long brown hair a little flat, so I sprayed some sea salt in it for texture and body. It seemed to do the trick, and I grabbed my coat, room key, and clutch purse before heading out the door.

I'd ended up ordering room service last night after I soaked in the tub and allowed my fantasies of Jase to take over. Dream Jase was an attentive lover, skilled in all things tongue- and finger-related. He ate me out like his life depended on it and fucked me senseless. Before I had known it, I had been climaxing, my fingers moving in and out of me as I called out his name and moaned into my otherwise empty bathroom.

Stepping into the warm and inviting lobby, I tried to rid my mind of all X-rated thoughts, feeling like Jase could not only read me like a book, but knowing that he'd call me out on it too. But all that flew out the window the second I spotted him near the massive white stone fireplace, a beanie covering his dark locks. How could a man look that good in simple jeans and a black jacket? He was downright fuckable without even trying.

His blue eyes snapped to mine, as if I'd said my thoughts out loud, and I tried to fight off the blush I knew was creeping into my cheeks. He didn't stay put and wait for me to reach him like most people would. No. The second Jase spotted me, his body moved, as if almost involuntarily, in my direction. Actually, the two of us headed toward one another like we were being pulled together by some invisible rope.

"Good morning, Val. You look beautiful," he said with a wicked gleam in his eye that I couldn't quite read. Before I could overanalyze it, he grabbed the back of my neck and pulled me in for a kiss.

OH MY GOD.

Jase was kissing me.

And I sure as hell was kissing him back.

My mouth opened for him like it wanted him there, like

his lips belonged attached to mine and nowhere else. And when his tongue pressed against my own, I swore my legs felt like they might give up and call it a day. How could they be expected to stand when he was kissing me like that?

My fingers dug into his shoulders for balance. He moaned into my mouth, his teeth tugging at my bottom lip as he pulled away with a pop.

"I just wanted to get that out of the way first," he said, his tone arrogant, confident, and hot as hell.

"Oh, so you're telling me that would have happened at some point then?" I pretended to question his judgment just to be combative.

"You and I both know it would have." His tone left no room for argument. There would have been no point anyway. He was right. We both knew it.

And I was glad he'd done it. Now, we could do it more. "Let's go."

He reached for my hand and pulled me out the revolving door into the chilly morning air, and I went with him blindly and willingly. I thought I might follow that man anywhere he asked me to.

Instead of questioning my judgment as frivolous and unsafe, I convinced myself that I was being adventurous and actually living a little for once. After all, I had looked him up online last night after we met, and he was exactly who he had said he was. I knew where he worked and scanned a few of his articles before pulling him up on all the social media platforms that I could find him on. For all intents and purposes, Jase Malone seemed fairly normal. And single.

To be on the safe side, however, I decided to send Karina an email, letting her know that I was planning on spending the day with him. I'd attached all of his personal information that I had accumulated online, including links and screenshots of pictures. You know, just in case seemingly *normal* Jase Malone was anything but and I disappeared and was never heard from again.

"You okay?" he asked, and I nodded.

I reveled in the feel of my hand in his, even through the gloves. His grip was firm, tight, and I liked feeling like he was holding on for dear life ... *to me*. When I looked at our glove-covered hands, my insides warmed, and tingles that I hadn't felt in years coursed through me.

The valet brought an SUV toward us before putting the car in park and hopping out.

"You drove here?"

"I prefer to have a car when I'm on an assignment. That way, I can go wherever I want, whenever I want, and I'm not limited in my options," he explained as he opened the passenger door for me and helped me inside.

Freaking gentleman. Like I needed to like him more.

The heater was blasting cold air at the moment, and I closed the vents before pressing the button to turn on my seat heater. Jase hopped inside and shivered.

"Cold as fuck in here," he swore before glancing at me, his eyes apologizing for the language even though I couldn't have cared less. Punching in an address into the car's GPS, he pressed Enter, and I watched the map come to life.

His hand reached over the center console and found my thigh before resting there, his fingertips digging into my skin. Long gone were the gloves, and I liked the way he wanted to touch me all the time. He made me feel wanted, and I realized that I hadn't felt like that in a long time. Desired. Sexy. Important.

Jase had made me feel more in twenty-four hours than Moore had made me feel in the last two years. The first year had been different. But we had also been young and consumed with each other before heading out into the real world.

Jase pulled the car out of the roundabout in front of the hotel and onto the main street.

"So, where are we headed first?" I asked with a smile as excitement prickled under my skin. Today's possibilities felt endless. Or maybe that was just how being with Jase felt.

"The oldest saloon in town." He grinned before adding, as if reading my mind, "Don't worry; there's food there."

"Thank God. I'm starving, and you did tell me not to eat." I placed my hand on top of his, and our fingers intertwined. *Have I ever felt so peaceful, so content?* I wondered to myself. Instead of getting inside my head, I relaxed, taking in the spectacular views that surrounded me. "So, tell me about this saloon."

Jase looked at me for only a second before focusing back on the road, pausing only to hear the navigation bark out orders every few minutes. "I don't know much about it. Like I said, this wasn't my assignment, and I didn't get that much time to research before I got here. Randy, my injured coworker, he had this meeting set up in advance, so I couldn't cancel. He has a very different reporting style than I do."

"Meaning?" I asked, wanting him to continue, to tell me about his style and how it differed from his broken coworker.

"Meaning that finding the oldest saloon in town is something that Randy would write about," he breathed out.

He sounded disappointed somehow, and I didn't get it.

"What's wrong with that? I think it sounds great. Genuine," I said, not seeing the issue.

The oldest bar in town, with so much history that it probably poured out of the wood it had been made with, sounded amazing. And as a tourist, it was something I would definitely want to see and experience—if I knew about it, that was.

"Nothing, but I bet every single travel writer who has ever come here has written about it. And I'm not saying it doesn't deserve to have the attention but"—he glanced at me—"I think we should be talking about the places that haven't been written about already. The things that you wouldn't think about."

His words sank into my bones and settled somewhere deep inside there. I totally understood what he was saying and couldn't even find it in me to argue. He had a point.

"Does that make any sense?" he asked, clearly mistaking my silence for some sort of judgment.

"Completely," I said, my tone serious as I squeezed his hand in mine. He squeezed back.

"I like to focus on things that are run or designed by the locals who actually live in the area. The last thing I want to do is write about the kind of places that are backed by big money. They don't need the extra publicity. Usually, the familiarity of their name gives them all the help they need. But small businesses don't have that luxury. Especially small businesses in small towns."

It felt like this man had opened up my mind and was peering inside at all my personal thoughts and opinions. I had the same exact feelings when it came to my little flower shop versus the large, coupon-discounting corporations online.

"I get it. I totally get it. How did you become so passionate about the little guy?"

His thumb rubbed against my skin, moving in a lazy up-and-down motion. I felt every single move his skin made against my own. "My parents owned a small jewelry store. But once the big-box store moved in down the street and sold anything anyone could ever need or want, my parents couldn't keep up. They couldn't match the prices, and even though the neighborhood wanted to support my family and keep them in business, it didn't make sense for them to pay twice as much for the same product. They lost the store, and it broke their hearts. Mine too."

My own heart ached in my chest from just hearing that story. I imagined what it must have been like for him to watch his parents lose everything they'd worked so hard for. And then I imagined what it would be like if that happened to me and my store. I'd be beyond devastated. Beyond destroyed. I'd have no heart left.

"Sorry, I didn't mean to get so depressing."

"You didn't. And I respect what you're doing. As a business owner, it's really hard to compete, and I can imagine how frustrating it must be to continually be overlooked if, say, you're the second-oldest saloon in Vail," I said with a slight laugh, "instead of the first one."

"You know, I never asked you what you did for work," he mentioned casually, and I'd known this question was coming.

I hesitated for only a second before I blurted out, a little too excited, "I own a flower shop!" I felt the smile take up my whole face. I loved what I did. I was proud of it, lived for it, and refused to lose it.

"Yeah? Really?" His face lit up too, like he was surprised and impressed, all rolled into one.

"Really. Going on three years now."

"Val, that's amazing. Is it successful?" He gave me a weird look before adding, "Sorry, that was rude. I just meant, is it hard to compete with the big-name floral shops and online sites?"

I shook my head. "Yes, and no. The one thing they have that I don't is money on a grander scale. Which means they have the ability to run huge marketing and promotional campaigns that I can't afford to run. But they're also nation-wide, and I'm not. So, in essence, they're competing with every flower shop in every state, and I'm only competing locally. They can never provide the kind of one-on-one customer service that I can. I think there's something special about knowing your customers by name and having an actual store that they can walk into, so they can see and pick their flowers instead of viewing pictures online."

"Pictures that end up looking nothing like the actual flowers that get delivered," he added with a frown.

"Exactly! I mean, who offers sunflowers year-round? It's not even possible. But people don't know that. They think if there's a picture with sunflowers in it, then that's what they're sending. But, hello, sunflowers don't grow in the winter."

Jase laughed. It was deep and throaty and masculine. "I agree wholeheartedly with everything you just said. Especially about the sunflowers. Maybe I'll convince my boss to let me do an article on your shop."

I let out an awkward laugh. "Oh, right. I'm sure your big, fancy magazine doesn't care about my tiny, local store."

I started to get nervous. Whatever this thing between us

was, it would only last for the weekend. At least, that was what I had assumed, and that was as far into the fantasy my brain had let me go. Him talking about writing up my store meant that we'd see each other again. Back home. In the real world. I wasn't sure that was even what I wanted.

Was I ready to jump into something again? I'd been single for, like, two seconds. Maybe Jase was just trying to be nice, and he wasn't even thinking about any of this like I was.

"What's going on in that head of yours?" he cut through my inner noise and asked.

I tossed him a small frown. "Who says anything is? Maybe I'm a blank canvas. Nothing going on in here." I knocked on the side of my head like it was made of wood.

"You make a face when you're lost in thought," he mentioned casually, as if that wasn't something that took most people months to figure out.

But I was quickly learning that Jase wasn't most people.

And I had no idea if I liked that or not.

GOLDEN BEARS

AFTER MEETING WITH the owners of the first original saloon, we spent the rest of the afternoon going to various stores on a list Jase had made, which were off the beaten path. As I watched him, I understood what Jase had meant. He asked questions that most wouldn't think of, and I knew he was searching for just the right angle for his writing. The right kind of hook that would make people actually want to go out of their way and leave their resort to visit these places.

He asked personal questions, learned their history, and by the time we left, I felt invested in every store owner we had met. I cared about their success. I wanted them to succeed.

Jase did that. He had made me feel that way.

"You're really good at this," I said as we got into the

car, my nose feeling like it might fall off. I was so cold.

His steel-blue eyes looked through me as he leaned over the middle console and kissed my lips. Every time he did that, I felt a jolt of surprise tear through me. He was exhilarating.

"Good at what? And I'm not fishing for a compliment either. I truly am asking."

"You're good at making people feel important. Like what they do matters. You made those owners feel valued. And you made me want to support them," I explained as he pulled off his beanie and ran his fingers through his messy hair. "Not everyone can do that."

I swore I saw him start to blush, and I wondered if I'd somehow embarrassed him.

"Thank you. That means a lot." He sounded so sincere.

"Do you know what you're going to write about?" I asked as he navigated the roads back to our hotel.

"I'm still working on it. I think so. I just want to firm something up." He glanced at me for a quick second. "You up for walking around the shops by the hotel?"

It wasn't like I had anything better to do than to spend more time with this sexy man. "Definitely," I said, sounding enthusiastic, and his face lit up.

"Good. Then, maybe we can grab dinner at one of the

more tourist places and see how it compares to where we just were," he directed.

"I'm actually interested to see how the stores around our hotel contrast to the ones farther away," I started to explain. "I feel like the resort shops will be"—I paused for a second while I picked the right word—"fancier? Bougier? Snobbier?" I added with a laugh. "That sounds rude, but it's not what I mean."

"No, I get it. I don't think you'll be wrong."

We dropped off Jase's car at the valet and hopped out, ready to explore some more. Jase stepped to my side and wrapped an arm around me without asking. He held me that way as we headed into the main strip of shops. Instead of pulling away or giving him some smart-ass quip, I leaned into his body, liking the way his arm felt around me. Like I belonged there. With him.

"I feel like we're in another country," I said as I looked around at the style of the shops.

"I know. It's very European."

"Have you been to Europe?" I asked, assuming that he had. He was a travel writer after all. As I waited for his response, the pangs of pain I expected to feel, knowing that Moore had dumped me for London, never came. If I'd thought I might despise all things Europe because of him, I would have been wrong.

"I've been all over," he answered even though it was sort of a non-answer.

"What's your favorite place?"

He sucked in a breath as he glanced up at the sky while we trudged forward slowly. I figured Jase would shout out his response before convincing me why I should go there too. But he stayed pensive and quiet, like I had asked him the hardest question in the world.

"I really don't know," he finally said.

"Really? Why?"

"Because every place I've been to is so different. I've loved them all for various reasons."

"Give me an example," I nudged, wanting to hear more of the way he thought.

He grinned as he looked down at me for only a second. "Okay. For example, Paris was my first overseas assignment, so I have a soft spot for it. It's not necessarily my favorite, but since it was my first, it's filled with fond memories. I think of Paris and smile."

"Everything you say sounds like a dream," I said before feeling a little naive and wishing I could take the thought back.

"I like that." He unwrapped his arm from me and

reached for my hand instead. *"Travel is like a dream.* I might put that in my article. Let's go in here."

He pointed at a jewelry store, and my legs almost gave out. Talk about being triggered. My breaths started coming at me rapidly, and before I knew it, I was bent over at the waist, Jase rubbing circles on my back, telling me to breathe.

"I'm sorry," he said. "I wasn't thinking."

"No." I waved him off as I took two more breaths and then stood upright completely. "I had no idea that would happen. I feel stupid."

"Don't say that," he snapped. "Your idiot boyfriend broke up with you instead of proposing. It's almost Valentine's Day. Of course a jewelry store was a bad idea on my part."

I swallowed hard as my breathing started to even out. "Why do you want to go in there anyway?" I asked because what guy in his right mind wanted to walk into a freaking jewelry store days before Valentine's?

"There's a story here about golden bears. This is the original shop that makes them, and Vail sort of adopted it as their symbol. I wanted to see them in person," he explained calmly, and I should have known that he had a logical reason for wanting to go inside.

"Golden bears? I'm intrigued." I started to perk up. I had no idea what a golden bear was, but I was ready to find out. "What are you waiting for?" I shot him a look before heading through the single glass door, the bell jingling just like my flower shop at home.

Jase followed close behind me, swatting my ass as he stepped inside. We were far too comfortable with one another to be strangers. But every time I started to feel like we were more than friends, I reminded myself that we'd only just met and this was a weekend fling. No sooner did the thought cross my mind than I got a text from Karina.

Worried that something might be wrong at the store, I opened it quickly, excusing myself to a corner of the jewelry boutique. I should have known better.

#1: ARE YOU ALIVE?

#2: PLEASE TELL ME YOU'VE TOUCHED HIS PENIS BECAUSE OMG, VAL, AFTER RESEARCHING HIM AND READING ABOUT HIM ONLINE, I WANT TO TOUCH HIS PENIS. TOUCH IT. PUT IT IN YOUR MOUTH!

I swore my face turned beet red as I looked up to make sure no one could read her words over my shoulder.

THERE HAS BEEN NO PENIS-TOUCHING. HOW'S THE STORE?

WHO CARES ABOUT THE STORE?! (UGH, IT'S FINE.) TELL ME ABOUT HIS PENIS. OR THOSE LIPS. I MEAN, PLEASE TELL ME YOU'RE FUCKING MOORE RIGHT OUT OF YOUR SYSTEM WHILE I SIT HERE AND COUNT THE MINUTES UNTIL YOU'RE BACK, GIVING ME EVERY SORDID DETAIL. I NEED THIS, VALERIE!!!

Ooh, she used my full name. That meant Karina was serious. I laughed.

Aside from the few times that Moore had come up in conversation, he rarely even entered my mind since I'd been here. I thought that was odd, to be honest. Heck, this whole weekend had been weird. Coming here at the last minute, meeting Jase, feeling like I'd known him forever when it had only been maybe twenty-four hours.

There was a small part of me that felt like this was all going to crash down around me. Maybe I hadn't been grieving Moore and the death of our relationship because I'd been distracted with Jase. And I wasn't sure how healthy that was. Was I simply biding my time before the reality of what I'd lost hit me like a rogue wave and pulled me under?

"Everything okay?" Jase asked, and I almost jumped, forgetting that I wasn't alone with my thoughts, but in the corner of a very busy store.

"Yeah, sorry. My coworker at the store." I waved my

phone in front of his face before pocketing it and ignoring Karina's last text.

"Is the store all right?" He was genuinely concerned. Jase cared about the well-being of my store.

"Yep. She was just checking in," I said, hoping that my cheeks weren't still flushed.

"Come here. I want to show you this." He reached for my hand again, like he'd done it a thousand times before, and pulled me toward a counter in the back, where a woman waited.

"There she is," the lady said as we reached her. "You two make a lovely couple." Her eyes practically twinkled as she looked at us.

Before I could argue or say that we weren't together, Jase responded with a simple, "Thank you," and I swore my ice-cold body started thawing out instantly. "She was telling me that the original bears were made here. And there was only one design. Now, there are many, a whole collection, but the first golden bear is rare. And the families here pass theirs down from generation to generation," he explained, and I felt the smile on my face grow, just listening to him tell the story.

"That's so cool," I said as I looked at the simple bear design. It reminded me of something you might see drawn on a cave wall. But there were so many different styles and jewelry types—from diamonds to stones. "I love that." I pointed at the two-tone bear necklace. The chain was in silver, but the bears were made of gold. They had a matching bracelet, too, but I couldn't wear things on my wrists at work; it got in the way of the flowers.

"That's from our newest collection. It's very popular," the woman said.

Jase thanked her for her time as he took a few photographs of specific pieces and promised to give the store credit if he mentioned them in the article. She was pleased, seemingly knowing that he couldn't possibly write about Vail without mentioning the bears.

Jase held the door for me as we walked back into the cold and stopped, plotting what to do next. New York was brisk, too, but this was a bitter mountain chill that went straight to your bones. "Honestly, that was the only store I wanted to see. Unless you wanted to do some shopping?"

I almost laughed. I wasn't really a big shopper. If we were talking about flowers and things for the store, I was all in and could spend way too many hours doing that. But shopping for myself wasn't really my thing. "I'm good. I do want to get my best friend and my employees a little something, but I can look in the gift shop at the hotel for that."

I wasn't sure what it was about hotel gift shops, but I freaking loved them. They had exactly what you needed when you were looking for local gems to bring home.

"Speaking of," Jase started to say as he looked me in the eyes, "I know I said we should go eat somewhere more touristy, but what do you think about going back to the hotel for dinner and drinks instead?"

I felt high just from him being so close to me.

I leaned up on my tiptoes and pressed a kiss to his mouth. "I think that's a great idea. You're going to write about the hotel, right?" I asked, and he nodded. "Well then, we need to eat there, so you can include the food in your article. We already know the drinks are fabulous," I added with a grin. "And we can visit the gift shop!" I said with a little too much enthusiasm that it made him laugh.

"Gotta tell you, Val, I don't want to leave your fucking side for a second, but I'm tired of lugging around my camera equipment. I want to go drop it off in my room and take a quick shower. Do you mind?"

What did he just say? Dear sweet Baby Jesus. Pull it together, Val. You're fine. Nothing to see here.

"No. That sounds heavenly. I'm actually freezing. Why is it so much colder here than back home?"

"Zero humidity," he said matter-of-factly before

wrapping me in his arms and heading back toward our hotel.

The heat hit my body once we stepped through the doors, and I felt my shoulders relax. I hadn't realized how tense the chill was making me. I spotted the gift store and forced myself not to run over toward it. I still had time to visit it and get the perfect gifts for my staff before I left.

"I'll see you in thirty? I can't wait any longer than that." Jase dropped a kiss to my cheek before pressing the elevator button.

"Meet you here?" I asked, feeling like I was about to embark on a first date of sorts.

"I'll be waiting," he said before the doors swung open, and I stepped inside … alone.

"You're not coming?"

"I'm on the first floor." He gave a slight head nod to the right, and I mouthed, *Oh*. "Thirty minutes, Val. Or I'm coming to find you."

The doors closed as nerves ripped through my body with anticipation. I wondered briefly what the rest of the night might hold as I walked into my room and closed the door behind me. I definitely considered sleeping with him as I picked out my cutest pair of matching bra and panties and slid them on.

Eat your heart out, Jase Malone.

DINNER & DRINKS

W ELL, HELL. I'D done my best to make sure Jase's jaw dropped open the second he saw me, but I practically tripped on my tongue at the sight of him. He'd dressed up for me. At least, I assumed it was for me. The man was a feast, and I was looking for a bite.

"You look stunning," he said, wrapping his hand in my hair and running his fingers through it. I prayed they wouldn't get caught.

"You look good enough to eat," I said, hoping I wasn't drooling as I bit on my bottom lip.

He leaned toward me. "I think I'm supposed to say that to you."

I wasn't even sure why I'd packed the red dress I was currently wearing in the first place, but I was grateful I had.

"Oh, Mr. Malone. Your table's ready," the hostess from

the night before said as soon as we were in her view.

We walked toward a private table for two, and I noticed the three large roses sitting in the center. They were perfectly pruned, not a natural thorn in sight. The buds were as big as my fist, and the color was the purest white I'd ever seen. They looked like snow.

"These are stunning," I said as I leaned forward to breathe them in.

"I'm glad you like them. I was a little scared they wouldn't live up to your standards," Jase said as I glanced around at the other tables, noticing that there were no other roses serving as centerpieces.

"You got these?"

He nodded. "I did."

"How?" I asked, seriously impressed.

Moore had never gotten me flowers. He said that there was no point in getting the woman who owned a flower shop ... more ... *flowers*. That he could never pick something that would be good enough when I criticized every other flower that wasn't from my shop.

I always thought it was the most absurd excuse ever, but he gave the same exact speech so many times over the years that I eventually believed him. But what a crock of shit. He never bought me flowers because he didn't want to. Plus, he could have asked Karina to get some, and he'd never done that either.

"I had help." He gave a soft smile in the direction of the hostess.

"I think you might be good at this whole hotel and romance thing," I said, reaching across the table for his hand and holding it. "Thank you. Really. They're gorgeous."

"I want to say something like how they aren't as gorgeous as you are, but that sounds cheesy, even in my head."

The heat crept up my cheeks, and I knew I was blushing ... *again*. Jase stirred up more feelings in me than I'd felt in years for anything other than flowers. "It's actually sweet."

We each ordered different drinks than we'd had last night—for the sake of research, of course—and when they arrived, they were just as visually stunning as the others.

I took a tentative sip before my eyes widened. "So good," I said, and Jase swirled his glass carefully before breathing in the scent and taking a small sip.

"Mine too." He nodded before licking his lips.

After looking at the menu for long enough that our waiter had stopped by twice, asking if we were ready, I still had no idea what to order. Everything sounded so good; I wanted to try it all.

"Having trouble?" Jase asked, and I looked up to see him watching me with a smirk on his face.

"How long have you been staring at me?" I buried my face, embarrassed that I was unable to make a decision.

His hand reached for mine and pulled it down, taking away my ability to hide. "Let me," he said.

I gave him a look. "Let you what?"

"Let me order for us both," he suggested, sounding confident.

I found myself liking the idea of him choosing my meal a bit too much. It was an old-school offer, archaic even, but for whatever reason, it felt more romantic than anything else.

Folding my menu in half and putting it down in front of me with a smile, I agreed, "Yes. You choose. I eat everything."

He grinned and reopened his menu for one last look before signaling for the waiter. He proceeded to order for us both like he was a regular here even though we both knew he wasn't. The waiter told him that they were excellent choices before hurrying off.

"To an unexpected weekend," Jase said, raising his glass toward me.

I reached for mine and clanged it against his, repeating

his words, "To an unexpected weekend."

We both sipped our drinks at the same time, fighting smiles as we did so. I hoped the liquid wouldn't drip down my mouth as I stared at his blue eyes and swallowed.

"These drinks are so damn good," I practically moaned in pleasure.

"They're totally on par with something we could get back home."

"Only in the hipster bars." I lifted a finger in objection, and he let out a gruff laugh.

"True, true." He grinned. "Val." My name sounded like velvet whenever he said it, smooth and sensual.

"Yes?"

"Tell me what went wrong in your relationship." He folded his hands and rested his chin on them. "I mean, I know I haven't known you that long, but I don't get it."

"Don't get what?" I bristled a little.

"Why someone would leave you after three years. That's long enough to know whether or not you want to marry someone. Did you not see it coming?"

I leaned back, my throat feeling constricted as Jase forced me to think about things that I hadn't even taken the time to analyze on my own yet. "I didn't see it coming," I said, a little defensive because that particular question made me feel stupid.

"I wasn't trying to upset you, Val," he said, and I could tell he felt bad.

"I know." I took another sip of my drink. Maybe for the confidence or the looseness the alcohol would eventually make me feel—I wasn't sure which. "I feel like I should have seen that we weren't really growing together as much as we were growing alone."

"What do you mean?"

"We were both focused on our career goals. I mean, we always had been. Even in college," I explained. "It had been that way for so long that I didn't realize we weren't trying to move forward as a couple as much as we were as individuals." I shook my head. "Does that even make sense?" I asked, my thoughts all jumbled up inside my brain.

"It does." He nodded. "And I get it."

I realized that I had been telling Jase a lot of personal information about me, but I didn't know anything about his past. "What about you?"

"What about me?"

"Have you ever been married?" I wasn't sure why I'd asked that particular question instead of something easier, but it was already out of my mouth.

Jase downed the rest of his drink. "I was actually

engaged once."

I tried to tamp down my surprise but knew it was written all over my face. "Really? Was it recent?" I hated thinking that it was. And I had no business feeling that way, all jealous and competitive. Jase hadn't been mine then. And he wasn't mine now.

"No." He shook his head. "We were young. I was stupid. Naive. A jerk really. Thank God we didn't go through with it."

"How old were you?" I asked, finishing off the rest of my drink as well, right as two fresh ones appeared.

"Nineteen."

"What?" I practically spat.

"I know. We were high school sweethearts, and I was immature. I didn't want her to go away to college, so I did the idiot thing and proposed."

"You proposed, so she wouldn't leave town?" I asked, feeling somewhat indignant on her behalf.

"Yeah. But her parents were smarter than we were and forced her to go off to college anyway. Said if what we had was real, we had nothing to worry about."

"Damn," I said, thankful for smart parents and kids who actually listened to them.

"It would have been a colossal mistake."

"And there hasn't been anyone since?" I asked, holding my breath for his response.

"I've dated on and off. Nothing serious though. I'm not sure why." He offered with a shrug. "I guess traveling and my work have always come first. Kind of like what you were talking about."

"I understand. I mean, my business comes first for me too. It has to. I'm the boss."

Being the owner of a brick-and-mortar store that also had employees meant that I was responsible for more than just myself. It wasn't just me that I had to look out for. Other people counted on me to provide for them, to make sure that they got a paycheck twice a month.

Jase leaned his body across the table between us, his lips moving so close to mine that I thought he might kiss me. "Do you come home at night, smelling like roses?" he asked in a whisper.

A laugh escaped. "I do actually."

The waiter cleared his throat, and both Jase and I jumped in response as he started placing the appropriate plates in front of each of us. I didn't realize how hungry I had been until the food appeared in front of me. Digging in, I didn't think I actually spoke a word until my plate was cleaned. I'd literally eaten every last bite.

"There's something sexy about a woman who actually eats," Jase said as he wiped his mouth with a napkin.

"What can I say?" I shrugged. "I like food. I am a New Yorker after all." As if that explained everything, but it really kind of did. If you came from a big Italian family, you'd understand. All we did was eat.

"Let's get out of here," he suggested before telling the waiter to put the cost of the meal on his room. I opened my mouth to complain, but Jase put a firm hand up. "Don't. This was my treat."

The whole day had been his treat. Jase hadn't let me pay for a single thing, and even though I knew this morning's activities were most likely going to be expensed through his company, I also realized that this meal would be kicked back from corporate accounting. I'd heard Moore complain about that enough times to know by heart what could and couldn't be expensed legally.

"Where do you want to go?" I asked as I stood up from my seat and put a hand on my way-too-full belly.

"Your room." He reached for my hand and started pulling me out of the restaurant, carrying the vase of white roses with his other hand.

I followed him willingly.

NO EXPECTATIONS

WITH EACH STEP out of the restaurant and toward the elevator in the lobby, I started second-guessing myself and my decisions. Even the alcohol coursing through my veins wasn't helping. What the hell was I doing?

It wasn't that I didn't want Jase.

I did. I really, really did.

But it felt sort of wrong. Like I was being foolish or acting like a love-struck teenager instead of a levelheaded woman who carefully measured all aspects of her life. I was jumping way too fast for someone typically so logical, someone who was usually scared to jump in the first place in regard to anything heart-related. I weighed out the pros and cons. Sometimes, I'd make a list before I agreed to go on a first date.

When the doors opened with a ding, Jase pulled me inside and pressed his body against mine before asking me which floor, his blue eyes watching mine with intent. He pushed the button, his focus still on me like I was his prey and he was my predator. I had nowhere to go, the wall of the elevator stopping me as he moved even closer.

"I can see your wheels spinning, Val." His breath skirted across my lips, and I forced my eyes to stay open instead of closing the way they wanted to.

"It's irritating how easily you read me," I complained.

"Listen to me carefully," he started to say, and I stared at his mouth, memorizing the fullness of his lips. "I know you don't typically hook up with strange men."

I tried to stifle a laugh but failed.

"It's okay to want me the same way I want you." He ran his hand down the length of my arm, causing goose bumps to rise. "It's okay to be attracted to me, to give in to what we have between us. We aren't doing anything wrong. We're two consenting single adults."

"I know that," I argued but was still a little uncertain.

"Do you? 'Cause I'm not sure you do."

I was a grown-ass woman, for God's sake, and it was

my body. I could do whatever I chose to with it. I just never had before. I'd always been in long-term relationships, and I'd never cheated or strayed.

"I've never had a one-night stand," I admitted, almost feeling like I'd missed some unwritten rite of passage in life.

"Neither have I," he said with a smirk.

"Liar," I countered, and he laughed.

"You're right. That was a lie. But I don't run around the country, doing this kind of thing either. It's happened once or twice, but I don't make a habit out of sleeping with random women," he explained.

Before he'd started talking about it, I hadn't even considered it.

What if I was one of hundreds of women? What if this was all some kind of charming act just to have sex with me? Before I could ask him, the doors opened, arriving at my floor, and he stepped out first, extending his hand toward me.

"What's wrong?" he asked as I ignored his hand and walked out on my own.

"Well, now, all I'm thinking about is how many strange Vs your P has been in."

His head cocked back. "How many what my what?"

I waved him off as I started toward my room. Even with

all the mixed signals I was throwing out, I was still currently leading us right to where my bed was located. "How many vaginas you've been inside. You have me thinking this is a bad idea. And that I'm probably, like, number one thousand or something and …"

My body stopped moving forward with the force of his arm on mine, holding me back. "You are not number one thousand. Or even one hundred. I'm not that type of guy," he said before gripping my neck and kissing me. Once he pulled away from my lips, he continued talking, "We don't have to do anything you don't want to do. Don't get me wrong; I want to savor every fucking inch of your spectacular body. But I understand if you're not ready to be consumed."

What in the ever-loving hell kind of speech was that?

My mind was a contradicting, jumbled mess. The devil on my shoulder wanted nothing more than to get tangled up in the sheets with Jase while the angel chastised that this was happening at warp speed and maybe I should slow down. I flicked the angel right off, hoping she fell and broke a leg or something as we reached the door to my room.

He kissed me again. His hands fisted in my hair, and I swore I felt a switch inside my brain flip off. I stopped caring about how many times he'd done this before or if it was the right thing to do or not. All I knew was that I wanted this man inside me, and I was damn well going to enjoy every moment.

Pulling away from his touch, I pressed my key card against the black pad of the lock. "Get in here," I demanded as the green access light lit up and the door unlatched with a click.

He placed the vase of roses on top of the desk before stalking toward his claim. Jase was all over me, his fingertips grazing my jaw, his eyes devouring me as if they could taste me just by looking. "I can't get enough of you," he whispered, but it sounded strained, forced almost, and it was sexy as hell.

"That makes two of us," I said as I reached for his pants and started unzipping them. Gripping the hem of his pants and his boxer briefs, I pulled them both down as I dropped to my knees and inspected the length of him before taking him in my fist. My eyes rolled in the back of my head at his soft, warm skin in my hand. I took him in my mouth before he could stop me, complain, or say a single word.

Jase's moans filled the room. He stood perfectly still, not thrusting or forcing himself any deeper inside me, and I loved that he allowed me to have all the control. I focused on sucking him off with the right amount of suction while moving my hand up and down at the base of his balls. He moaned again, louder this time, and I knew he liked what I was doing to him.

It felt powerful, having him in my control like this. Maybe it should have felt the opposite, considering the fact that I was the one on my knees, but I knew that as long as he was in my mouth, I held all the cards. I liked the way it felt.

"Val." His voice strangled out of him, and I stopped sucking with a pop. Strong hands reached for my shoulders and pulled me to my feet. "You can't keep doing that."

I didn't ask him to explain or tell me more. I knew what he meant. He leaned down and pulled his pants back in place, which was a damn shame, before his fingertips tilted my chin upward to look at him. His eyes were unreadable as he planted a kiss against my lips. It was softer than I knew how to interpret, almost loving, and I tossed that thought right back out of my head as quickly as it had entered.

"Can I turn on the fire?" he asked, moving toward the gas fireplace in the corner of the room.

"Yeah."

I watched as he flipped the switch on the wall, and the fire came to life with a small roar. The mood had already been set, but this definitely added to it.

"On the bed." Jase's tone of voice surprised me, and I shot him a look. "You heard me, Val."

"Damn," I said but then promptly did what I had been told.

As I sat on the edge of the bed, still fully clothed, Jase stalked toward me before doing exactly what I had done a few minutes earlier—he dropped to his knees to worship me.

"My turn." He winked before reaching for the bottom of my dress and shoving it upward.

Those deep blue eyes took every inch of me in appreciatively, his breath catching as more and more of my legs were revealed. I'd never felt so sexy before in my entire life.

I thought about saying something teasing, but his head dived between my legs and his fingers pulled my panties to the side and I couldn't say anything at all, let alone think. The second his tongue licked me, I short-circuited, completely lost in the moment. It felt so good. My body fell backward onto the bed, my back arching as my breathing became erratic. Fisting his hair, I pulled at it before moving to his ears and doing the same, wanting more of what he was giving.

Everything Jase did was so pleasure-filled; I really thought I might die from it.

"You're so good at this," I said with a shaky breath, and he stopped for a moment to look at me. I almost killed him. "Oh my God, don't stop," I whined, and he gave me a smirk before diving back down and finishing the job.

My body was racked with ecstasy, coming down from the high he'd given when he finally rose back to his feet. He reached out a hand to me, and I took it. Pulling me to a stand, he spun me around until my back was facing him, and he reached for the zipper on my dress and tugged it all the way down. I stepped out of it, wearing nothing but the matching bra and panty set I'd picked out earlier. Jase made short work of his clothes, tossing everything into a pile on the floor, except for his charcoal-gray boxer briefs. That man's body was a sight to behold, chiseled and filled out in all the right places.

"Like what you see?" He gave me a slight nod, and I laughed.

"Damn right I do." My eyes practically bulged out of my head.

"I love what I see."

Jase stepped toward me, one arm reaching for my waist. He pulled me against him and unhooked my bra and dropped it to the floor before I even realized he'd done it. He went to work on my thong next, looping his fingers around the flimsy material and tugging it down until I kicked it off completely. He did the same with his boxer briefs before directing me back onto the bed.

I had no idea what I expected sex with Jase to be like, but slow, methodical, or gentle definitely wasn't it. For some reason, I'd always figured that a one-night stand would be more like tossing each other into walls, breaking pictures from knocking them over, resulting in bruises you couldn't remember getting.

But Jase entered me like he'd never get the chance to do it again. He took his time, his fingers tracing the curves of my body like a Sam Hunt song, and by the time he was finished, not a single cell on me had been left untouched. He worshipped me in ways I hadn't even known were possible, made me feel things sexually I'd only ever read about.

And when we showered together, he fucked me again, this time from behind, pounding into me so hard that I thought we might break something. His fingers left marks on my thighs. My hips were sore from his grip. And if I had to do this night all over again, I'd say yes ten times out of ten.

Jase Malone was the best sex I'd ever had.

I WOKE UP the next morning, sore in all the right places, my body exhausted in the best of ways. When I rolled over, I noticed the bed was empty. Relief and disappointment battled for my top feeling as I touched his pillow, noting that it was cold. I'd allowed myself to get caught up in the moment last night, and I'd enjoyed every second of it, but the harsh light of a new day had a way of erasing all that. It reminded me that I had just ended a three-year relationship and should be in some state of mourning, not in bed with someone else. The switch that had shut off in my mind had definitely been turned back on.

Sitting up, I tucked the covers under my arms and ran a hand through my hair just as a knock on the door startled me. It started to open, and I almost screamed to housekeeping that I was inside *and naked*, but Jase's head appeared instead.

"I borrowed your key." He waved it around as he walked through the door, balancing a bag and a crate of coffees.

He hadn't left me during the middle of the night, like I'd thought. The jerk had gone out for food and caffeine, still wearing the same clothes he'd worn at dinner.

A part of me hated how thoughtful and romantic he was. Mostly because I knew there was no point to his kind gestures. We'd never see each other again. But maybe that was what made it all so easy—no expectations. Jase seemed perfect because he only had to maintain the illusion for a few days, not a lifetime, like real relationships.

He set up the food and coffee on a tray and placed it on top of the bed before settling back in next to me.

"You're a god," I said as I reached for the coffee and took a tentative sip. There was nothing more awful than burning your mouth.

"I've heard worse." He sipped his own drink before taking a muffin and tearing at it, handing half to me. "So, Val, is this how you imagined spending your time in Vail?"

I almost choked. "Um, no. I definitely didn't plan on meeting anyone while I was here."

"Is that a good or bad thing?" Jase was fishing for a compliment. Or maybe he was simply trying to read my emotions, but I wasn't giving in.

"Still deciding," I teased.

"Harsh."

"Joking," I said, a little uncomfortable. "But really, I figured I'd be alone and soul-searching—or whatever people are supposed to do after a breakup. You know what I mean?"

He nodded. "I know what society says you're supposed

to do. But I don't think there's a handbook every person should follow. We all heal in different ways."

I smiled. "I know you're just trying to make me feel better."

"I'm really not." He finished off his half of the muffin before reaching into the bag and pulling out a croissant. "Can I ask you something?"

"Of course."

"Do you feel guilty?"

Shaking my head, I swallowed hard. "No. I didn't do anything wrong, so I don't have anything to feel guilty about."

"But there's a part of you that thinks we were irresponsible, right?" His voice sounded genuinely sad.

"How do you do that?" I asked, irritated. It made absolutely no sense at all that this guy would be able to figure me out so easily, like I was some sort of open book that he was well versed in. And he'd been doing it since day one.

Jase shrugged. "I don't know. You're easy for me to read. Your emotions are written all over your face."

Snarling, I glared at him and shoved the rest of the muffin in my mouth. I couldn't talk if my mouth was full.

"I got a call this morning. I have to head back early."

My stomach dropped with his words. "How early?"

He glanced down at the watch on his wrist. "I leave for the airport in an hour."

"Oh." I knew I sounded disappointed, but I still had another full day here in Vail, and the idea of spending it alone wasn't at all appealing. The irony was not lost on me.

"You've been the best part of my trip," he said before clearing his throat. "Hell, you might be the best part of my whole year."

"It's only February," I said, my mouth still filled with starchy goodness. "Still a lot more months to go."

Jase pushed up from the bed and walked toward the massive balcony window. He pulled the curtain wider, and even more light filled the room. I watched him, knowing that something was going on inside that head of his, the same way he always knew what was going on with me.

"Say it already," I demanded.

He reared back to look at me. "Say what?"

"Whatever you're thinking about. Whatever you're not saying. Just say it."

He paced the room, and I watched him inhale slowly, like he was working up the nerve. Jase was nothing but confident, so seeing him vulnerable should have been off-putting, but it was sexy as hell.

"I was wondering," he started, his blue eyes meeting

mine and holding, "what would you think about us seeing each other again?"

"Again? Like when?" I knew exactly what he was getting at, but avoiding it like some sort of coward seemed like the right thing to do at the time.

"Don't do that." He sounded almost annoyed at my deflection. "Val, I want to see you when we get back home. We live in the same city. We both weren't even supposed to be here this weekend. This can't be that big of a coincidence. It has to mean something more."

I looked away from him. His stare was too intense. His body was too magnetic. I couldn't think straight when I looked at him. He clouded all my judgment. Plus, this wasn't New York. I had a life and a job and a business that depended on me. As long as I was in Vail, I had nothing but wide-open days and free time. We'd been playing house the past couple of days. This wasn't reality.

"I don't know," I said, my voice weak. "Don't you think it would be better to leave this here, where it belongs?"

"This isn't Vegas. What happened here doesn't have to stay here," he countered.

"I just ..." I wasn't sure how to tell him that part of the reason I'd been able to give myself to him so easily was the idea that I'd never have to see him again. I'd convinced myself that he was just a brief fling. If he was going to be more than that, I most likely would have run for the hills the second I sat down next to him at the bar that first day. At least, that was one of the many lies I seemed to tell myself when it came to him.

"Val," he said my name so softly. "Don't you think we've started something here?"

That was the million-dollar question. But what was real, and what was make-believe? And how could we tell the difference between the two?

"I don't want to ruin it."

"How could seeing each other again ruin it?"

"Because this has been the perfect past few days. I just want it to stay that way forever," I said, knowing that I'd never forget Jase as long as I lived, but he would soon become nothing but a memory that I would cherish.

Jase walked back to the bed and sat near me, his hand on mine. "I know you're scared, but there's a good chance that we could be perfect every single day. Not just while we're here."

I started shaking my head in disagreement. I'd thought I was right when I chose Moore, but I couldn't have been more wrong. My ability to read people was crappy at best. I didn't trust myself right now. Not when it came to relationships and definitely not when it came to Jase Malone.

"I can't," I whispered. "I'm not ready."

He pulled his hand away and stood back up. "Okay. I understand." The words didn't match his tone or his body language. "Well, I have to get going. It was nice to meet you."

I knew I'd hurt his feelings when he turned toward the door and walked straight out of it without saying another word or kissing me good-bye. Part of me wanted to sprint out of bed and chase after him, but I sat there instead, not wanting to spend another second in this town without him.

Jase Malone had ruined Vail for me.

TIME TO GO HOME

I CALLED THE airline and changed my flight for later that evening. It gave me time to go to the gift shop and pick up the presents I still hadn't gotten for Karina and the other employees. There was an earlier flight in the afternoon, but I assumed it was the one that Jase was on, and I couldn't fly back to New York with him and then walk away forever. I might be a strong woman, but I wasn't that strong.

Not to mention the fact that I was already mourning his loss more than my previous relationship. My mind should have been processing the fact that the future I'd thought I'd have with Moore was gone in a flash, but all it was thinking about was Jase. It was like Moore had never even existed. I had to force myself to think about him.

What the hell was wrong with me?

With my bags in hand, presents included, I headed for

the airport. And by the time I landed at JFK, the flower store had been closed for hours. I knew Karina would be at home and most likely still awake, so I headed straight to her apartment. I needed my best friend.

At her building, I pressed the intercom button for her apartment and heard her voice wearily ask, "Who is it?"

"It's me."

"Val? What the hell?" she shouted before the sound of a buzzer alerted me that the building door was unlocked.

I pulled it open before making sure it closed shut behind me and sprinted up three flights of stairs.

Karina was standing with the door open, a confused smile on her face. "You're not supposed to be back until tomorrow night. What happened? Did super-sexy Jase Malone do something? I know everything about him, Val. I can find him and inflict everlasting pain."

Smiling, I shook my head and launched into her arms, hugging her. "He was great. Too great actually. Now, let me in," I said before pushing my way past her body and into her tiny apartment.

She closed the door and turned to face me, one hand on her hip. "If he's so great, then why are you back early?"

"I'll tell you if you stop talking for two seconds." I plopped down on her couch and kicked my feet up on her coffee table.

"Hey," she complained before sitting down next to me. "Tell me everything. And I do mean, everything."

She suggestively wagged her eyebrows, and I almost told her nothing had happened. But we both knew I was a terrible liar.

"First, how's the store?" I asked because I needed to check in on my baby.

"It's great. No issues. No problems. Literally couldn't be more perfect." She held her hands up in prayer pose. "Promise. Now, talk."

Karina watched me, her eyes bugging out at times as I filled her in on almost every detail from the moment I'd met Jase until he left me in my hotel room. I'd never seen that look on her face before, and I suddenly felt exposed and a little judged. It made me uncomfortable.

"Why are you looking at me like that?"

A half-grin appeared on her face. "Because it's incredible. This is like something straight out of a movie! It's like a dream."

I stopped myself from laughing. She sounded so excited. "So, you don't think I'm crazy for sleeping with him?"

"What?" Her head practically spun off her shoulders at

my question. "No. Never. I told you to have a manventure! I meant it."

"But—" I started to say, and she cut me off with a wave of her hand.

"But nothing. People have one-night stands all the time. It doesn't make you a bad person." Her words struck an immediate chord. "You have to see him again. It's fate, Val."

"No. I can't," I complained, trying to tell her that seeing him again wasn't logical.

"Why not? Are you crazy?" She jumped up from the couch and started pacing back and forth. "He asked to see you. Which means he likes you. Why would you say no?"

I swallowed hard. I'd been thinking about exactly that during my entire flight back home. I spent so much time convincing myself that telling Jase no had been the right thing to do that I completely ignored what I'd actually wanted to say to him. My heart had leaped at the idea of seeing Jase again, but my brain had screamed *no* louder than it could take. It went into overdrive, listing reasons and making excuses that I bought into, while my poor ticker pleaded to be heard as well. Naturally, I'd ignored my heart and listened to my head because … well … logic.

"Don't you think I should be alone after being with someone for three years? Isn't that the right thing to do instead of jumping into something else so quickly?"

"I don't know. Probably. I guess. But ..." she said before stopping abruptly and sitting back down.

"But what?"

"But this guy sounds dreamy. Like he stepped out of a book and into your life."

"Of course he was dreamy. It was only a couple of days. Really easy to be the perfect guy when there isn't enough time to show your flaws."

Karina reared her head back and looked at me like I had grown another. "When did you get so cynical? That's my job."

Her words struck another nerve. I'd always been the romantic one. The one who believed in fairy tales and fate and true love.

"I don't know," I said honestly because I didn't.

Maybe Moore leaving had hurt more than I realized. Or maybe it'd hurt me in ways I hadn't put together yet. Our failed relationship had definitely made me question my judgment. And in that moment, it had also made me feel like I wasn't worth sticking around for. I'd never felt that way before now, but Moore leaving so easily had made me think I wasn't worth the fight. And if my boyfriend of three years could walk away like I'd meant nothing, what did that say about me?

"I don't like this side of you," Karina whined. "We can't both be cynics. And it was my job first."

I giggled. "It suits you better anyway."

She smacked her hand on the end of the couch. "Damn straight! Plus, you got dumped by the guy you'd thought you were going to spend the rest of your life with. There's no way that can't affect you."

"Jeez, Karina," I said because even though her words were the truth, they felt extra harsh.

"It's true. But it's not your fault, Val. You two had nothing in common, except your passion for work. Separate passions, I might add."

I sat there, quiet, soaking in the truth I'd already come to accept even if it was hard. "Screw Moore. Let's talk about Jase and how I'm going to start dating him if you won't."

She was teasing, and I knew it, but my body flared to life as jealous anger swirled in me.

Karina laughed and pointed. "Oh, you should see your face right now. You *like*, like him."

"I can't stop thinking about him," I admitted but quickly added, "but then again, I just left him."

"You are doing classic Val right now," she said as she rolled her eyes.

"What does that mean?" I asked, a little annoyed that I was being typecast.

"Talking yourself out of something because you don't want to do the wrong thing. You do this all the time. Except with the shop. You need to be as fearless in love as you are with your flowers."

I glared at her, not wanting to accept that this was my MO. "Give me an example then," I said, and she chewed on her bottom lip. "If I do this all the time, then tell me when."

"Fine," she said as she held up one finger. "One, when you didn't give your number to the super-hot drummer at the concert because you thought he'd be a bad influence. And good girls don't date guys in bands." She held up a second finger. "Two, when you said no to the fraternity formal with Dale because he was a baseball player and athletes are players on and off the field. He was such a nice guy, and you refused to give him a chance."

When she held up a third finger, I stopped her from adding to the list.

"I'm just saying, when it comes to guys, you talk yourself out of dating them. Lord knows how Moore even got past those defenses," she said with a slight laugh. "But you're doing it again with Jase. Because you think you should suffer more. Or that people will judge you for moving on so quickly."

"It's not that I think people will judge me," I started to explain. "I don't want to judge myself."

"What does that even mean?"

My thoughts rumbled around in my head as I tried to make sense of them all. "I feel like I'm supposed to analyze my relationship with Moore for some specific length of time or something before I move on."

"What?" Karina looked at me like I was a legit crazy person who needed to be locked up in a straitjacket. "How long? A week? A month? A year? What's the appropriate amount of time to grieve a three-year relationship ending that sucked anyway?"

I threw my hands in the air. "I don't know! But I'm sure it's longer than a freaking week. Shouldn't I be trying to figure out what went wrong, so I don't repeat the same mistakes?" I asked even though I had no idea why I was pushing this concept so hard.

"Here's what I think," Karina started. "I think that you're a good girl and a good person, Val. You think there's some set of rules you're supposed to follow after a heartbreak. But the truth is that there isn't. People will tell you to take your time. To stay single. To have a relationship with yourself first after getting out of one." She used air quotes around certain sentences and said the words like she was reading from some sort of script. "And that's fine if you want to do that. But it's also fine if you don't. Most people don't meet a great guy the second they break up with someone else. But you did."

I nodded along with her, liking what she was saying and how she was explaining it, when she asked, "Can I ask you something?"

"Of course."

"Do you even miss Moore? Like, truly. Or do you miss him because you think you're supposed to?"

The very concept was like acid in my belly. "I don't miss him. I miss Jase."

"That tells you everything you need to know. Idiot."

Maybe Karina was right. I was an idiot. I'd met this incredible guy, and I'd let him walk away and out of my life like I didn't care that he was going.

"Apparently, I needed to talk this out."

"Clearly. I'll send you my bill." She smiled before standing up from the couch and reaching for me. "Now, leave, so I can sleep. Unless you want to spend the night?"

"I would, but I need to go home. I'll see you tomorrow. You'd better not have hurt my flowers while I was gone," I chastised.

She laughed manically. "You'll never know."

Walking out of Karina's apartment building and into the chilly night air, I hailed a cab easily, hopping into the backseat before giving the cabbie my home address. He sped off down the road, and I closed my eyes until we stopped.

"We're here, miss," the driver's gruff voice said, basically waking me up.

"Thank you." I looked at the meter and gave him a twenty, telling him to keep the change before I exited the car with my suitcase.

Once I was inside my apartment, I felt simultaneously relaxed and fidgety. I was happy to be home, but a part of me felt like I'd rushed back here without thinking twice about it. Nothing had changed. Everything was still in the same spot where I'd left it. But for the first time in my life, I felt sort of out of place, and I wasn't sure why. That feeling made zero sense.

Tossing my suitcase onto my bed, I unzipped it and started to unpack. I wasn't the kind of person who could roll her luggage into a corner to deal with later. No, I was way too organized for that. I unwrapped the three white roses that I'd carefully packed, thankful that they hadn't broken apart during the flight. If they had, I would have put all the petals into a small jar to dry before bringing them to the shop, so I could stare at them all day. Yes, I'd brought the roses. How could I not? They'd mocked me from my hotel room, basically begging to come back to New York with me. Plus, I liked the memory. It made me feel special.

They were just as beautiful as they had been at dinner, so I grabbed a piece of string from my nightstand, tied them together at the ends, and hung them upside down from my curtain rod. They would dry perfectly that way.

I removed the bag of little presents that I'd gotten for Karina and the rest of my employees to bring to the shop tomorrow, and that was when I noticed it. A small white box I didn't recognize. I had no idea where it had come from or what it was, but I knew I hadn't put it in there.

Pulling it out, I opened the top and saw a familiar bear logo printed on a velvet pouch. My heart started pounding as I untied the bag and poured the contents into my palm. The silver-and-gold bear necklace that I had fallen in love with in Vail stared back at me. My jaw fell open, not only because I'd seen the price tag when we were in the store together, but also because I had no idea how he'd bought this without me noticing.

Tears pricked my eyes as I quickly put the necklace on. Wearing the gift made me feel closer to him somehow. Like

I hadn't just basically told him good-bye forever and to never contact me again. I reached for my phone to send him a thank-you text but put it down instead. I'd figure out exactly what to do about him tomorrow. Tonight, I needed to sleep on it all and see how I felt when I woke up in the morning.

Maybe now that I was home and had my flower shop to focus on, Jase Malone wouldn't even cross my mind.

JUST MY LUCK

I 'D BEEN BACK in New York for days, and even with the upcoming holiday and our plethora of orders, thoughts of Jase still hadn't left my mind. Every day, I'd been tempted to find him or at least reach out in some way. Knowing that he was so close drove me insane. Nights were the hardest. All the distractions of the workday were long gone, and memories of our time together replayed in my head on a loop.

The way he'd kissed me, touched me, made me scream out his name.

God, I missed it.

I missed him.

This guy I barely even knew was consuming my thoughts.

As the hours turned into days, it started feeling like I'd

missed my chance to reach out to him somehow. It would have been one thing if I'd called him right when I got back home, but seven days later felt like an eternity. What the hell would I even say?

I'd been a complete and utter idiot if I thought that Jase Malone was the kind of guy you met and simply got over. Pretending he never existed wasn't working. And when I'd previously shown Karina the necklace he'd bought me, I'd thought she was going to leave the store and come back with him on her back.

"You are being a fool. I just want it known. Do I need to repeat it? 'Cause I will say it again," she warned. "And again."

"I know," I agreed with her, but I was still adamant not to reach out.

Naive parts of me figured that if Jase missed me as much as I missed him, he would show up at my store and declare his love and sweep me off my feet. It was foolish and unfair, but I couldn't help still wishing for it to happen.

"Stop it," Karina chastised as she came around the corner and leaned against the counter.

"Stop what?"

"I know that look on your face. You want him to do something drastic to prove his love for you," she said, using air quotes again. "But that's not fair. You told him no. He's being a good listener."

"I thought guys didn't listen when they wanted something," I countered as she grabbed a pair of shears.

She pointed them at me. "That's only in books. And movies. In real life, they don't like to feel stupid."

Damn. "Do you think I made him feel stupid?" I asked, suddenly feeling awful and hating myself for making Jase feel anything other than talented and caring and amazing.

Karina let out a howl. "He practically begged to see you again, and you said no. No discussion. No maybe. No thinking about it. Straight-up no and then bye forever." She waved the shears in the air at an imaginary Jase.

"I don't like your CliffsNotes version of things," I whined.

"But it's true. He put himself out there. You shot him down. If you want the guy, you're going to have to go to him. Or jeez, Val, send him a text. It's not like you don't have his number." She stopped talking only long enough to take a breath before launching in again. "Did you even tell him thank you for that necklace you refuse to take off?"

I felt ashamed and embarrassed that I hadn't even done that. "No," I admitted softly.

"That's just bad manners. I'm telling your mom."

It was rude. And inconsiderate. Two things I normally never was.

"Look, Val, if you don't reach out to him, I will. I swear. I have all of his online information. You can't stop me," she threatened, and I knew her words weren't hollow. Karina would absolutely end this charade if I didn't do it myself, but I would be humiliated in the process.

"I can handle this myself." I gave her a pointed look. "And I will. I'll text him later."

"Promise?"

I nodded. "Promise. But first, I need lunch."

"Please go get us food. I'm starving, and your flowers want to eat my fingers—I know it."

EVEN THOUGH IT was cold outside, I decided to walk instead of taking a cab or heading down into the subway. The air reminded me of Vail, which, of course, made me think about Jase. Not that he wasn't constantly in my head already, taking up space without asking.

I rounded the corner and hoped that there wasn't a line out the door. If there was, I would stay anyway because this deli made the best sandwiches in twenty blocks and was worth the wait, but I'd left my jacket at the shop. Wrapping my arms around my sweater and pulling it tight, I breathed out in relief that there was only one person who looked to be standing outside. I could handle that.

The guy in front of me had his order written down on a piece of paper. I saw him holding it and stifled the groan from coming out. It was long. He must be picking up for his whole office or something.

"Are you just getting something for yourself?" he turned and asked, as if reading my mind.

"Oh, me and one other," I answered.

He stepped to the side. "Go ahead. I literally have twelve sandwiches to order."

"Really?" I asked, sounding surprised.

It wasn't that New Yorkers weren't friendly—we could be; it was just that we were always in such a rush. Our time was limited. Our days were packed. And giving people cuts in line at the most popular deli wasn't our usual MO.

"Really. Go before I check what time it is and change my mind," he said with a laugh.

I touched his shoulder and squeezed it. "Thank you so much. I really appreciate it."

Pulling open the front door, I stepped inside and stopped it from slamming behind me as I took in the hustle and bustle of the people working behind the counter. They moved like a choreographed dance, swirling out of one another's way while cutting fresh meat and shouting at the waiting customers. It made me smile, and the smell of freshly baked bread made my stomach growl.

My eyes roved the crowded space, pausing on a familiar shape, and my stomach stopped growling and dropped to my feet. Jase Malone was about twenty feet in front of me. I'd never once run into him before—that I knew of—and now, I was seeing him at my favorite deli on a random weekday. What were the odds?

I studied the back of his head and the width of his shoulders, knowing without a doubt that it was him. I would have bet money on it. He didn't even need to turn around and show me that gorgeous face of his for confirmation. My mouth opened to say his name, as I felt like this was fate somehow stepping in—again—when I realized that he wasn't alone.

A tall brunette cozied up to his side, and I watched as his arm fell to her lower back and stayed there. She leaned her head against his shoulder, and they stood together that way—comfortable, familiar, loving. I couldn't stop staring, my eyes blurring as I fought back the emotions that roared to life inside me.

I felt like a fool, and I had to get out of there before he

spotted me. My seeing him was one thing, but I couldn't actually face him and not cause a scene if he realized I was there. When I turned to leave, my eyes caught on something as Jase's date raised her left hand to rest it on his shoulder. The gem on her ring finger sparkled, even in the old fluorescent lighting, and I swore that I might be sick right then and there.

He was engaged?

I shook my head, my empty stomach threatening as I turned to get the hell out of there before I embarrassed myself and made a mess all over the black-and-white tiled floor. He'd lied to me. And he'd done it all so easily. The worst part was that I'd believed him without question.

Of course I'd believed him. I always told the truth, and I stupidly expected that other people did the same thing. Even when life had shown me otherwise, my default was to be trusting and to naively accept people at their word.

When would I learn?

I chastised myself as I rushed away from the nightmare replaying in my mind without any food. Not that I could have stomached eating at this point anyway, but Karina still needed something. She'd kill me if I came back empty-handed. I stopped at a pizza joint and grabbed a whole pie to go. It would have to do.

When I walked into the shop, pushing against the door with my hip, the bell jangled.

"Be right out," Karina shouted from the back.

"It's just me," I yelled, and she let out a whoop, excited for the food.

"Yay! Oh, pizza! I'm eating this whole thing," she warned as she opened the top, grabbed a slice, and folded it in half before I even set the box down. "Aren't you eating?" She looked at me with an odd expression as she took a huge bite. "Val, what happened?" She put her slice back down on top of the box.

My throat felt like I'd eaten a bucket of sand. "I saw Jase at the deli," I said, my voice monotone as I tried to keep my emotions from coming out.

"What?" Her eyes grew wide. "Wait. Why aren't you happy?"

"He wasn't alone," I said as I pulled out one of the barstools at our flower counter and sat.

She continued to chew her food, and I watched as she swallowed, contemplating exactly what my words meant. "He was with a girl?"

I nodded, my eyes instantly burning as I tried to hold back the tears. "Not just any girl," I stated. "She was wearing an engagement ring."

"Okay, okay." Karina waved me off with a breath. "So what? That doesn't mean she's *his* fiancée. She could have been anyone."

"They were holding each other," I added, and my hand went to my stomach. "I feel sick."

The bell rang, and we both turned to see a couple walking into the store, holding hands.

"I got this," Karina whispered toward me before ushering me into the back room, where I could pull myself together—or lose it completely in peace.

Nothing made sense. Jase hadn't seemed like the kind of guy to lie or cheat, but what the hell did I truly know about him? Spending forty-eight hours with a stranger didn't make me an expert on his character. I'd spent three years with a guy and felt like I didn't know him at all at the end. People only showed you what they wanted you to see.

Still, none of it added up. Why buy me the necklace? Why ask to see me again if he had a fiancée waiting for him at home? When we'd talked about our past at dinner, I'd never once gotten the impression that he was lying or being deceitful. But I couldn't ignore what I had seen. They looked like a couple. She had a ring on. He had his arm around her. And maybe he'd just wanted to get in my pants. It wasn't like guys didn't do that kind of thing all the time for sex.

"Okay, they're gone." Karina popped into the room, carrying the pizza box. "They wanted to buy flowers and the pizza. Can you believe that? Trying to take my food from me. Couldn't they see I was starving?"

I managed a laugh. "Why are all guys liars?"

"They're not," Karina argued.

I'd figured she would agree with me. She was the cynic after all.

"It doesn't make any sense though, right?" I asked, hoping that her insight might make me feel better or help things add up.

She shook her head. "It really doesn't. That's why I don't want to believe it. And why I'm not sure that you do."

"Because I saw them with my own eyes," I said, wishing I could bleach the scene from my memory. "I can't believe I slept with someone who has a fiancée. What kind of monster am I?"

"You didn't know."

"Do I find her and tell her?" I asked. Didn't I have some sort of obligation towards my fellow women to uphold? Wasn't there girl code for this type of thing?

"Oh, hell no. That is one cage fight you do not enter. Tap out, sister," Karina said as she focused on her phone and typed furiously before handing it to me. "Look. There are no pictures of him with any girls. And no pictures of him tagged with any girls either."

"I know," I said because I'd already checked his social media profiles the other night. I'd done a deep dive, going as far back as it allowed, like a proper psycho. "But if you notice, he hasn't had any tagged photos of him for the past three years. It's like he stopped them from showing up on his profile altogether. And his entire feed is his photographs for work. There's nothing personal on there at all."

"True," she agreed as she took her phone back and continued scrolling. "That's true. Ugh, I just refuse to believe this."

The bell jangled again, letting us know that another customer had entered the shop.

"Well, I don't have time to overthink it right now. Valentine's Day is just around the corner, and I have plenty of work to keep me busy and focused and help me forget all about him," I said, hoping that my brain would believe the lie even though my heart laughed at it.

"I'll go greet them. Come out when you're ready. You know the customers love you best."

Karina left the back room without another word, and I was so grateful to have her in my life.

But in the midst of all the thoughts spinning around inside me, I still couldn't believe just *how* hurt and disappointed I felt. How let down. It made me truly realize that I had wanted to see Jase again even though I'd told him that I didn't. I wanted the same things he did, but I'd been too afraid to admit it.

The unwritten rules of society had made me feel like jumping into another relationship right after ending one was wrong somehow. Like it made me a bad person. How could I move on so quickly and not expect to be judged by everyone? But society didn't even know me—or my heart.

I wasn't typically careless or frivolous.

I planned.

I researched.

I thought things out.

Jase was the first time that I'd jumped without a parachute. And I loved the thrill. But mostly, I loved being with him, how he looked at life and how he looked at me. No one had ever made me feel the way Jase Malone had.

But none of it had been real. It had all been a charade. And I had no idea how to reconcile all of those conflicting sentiments inside of me. I guessed that I was lucky to have a business to run. Nothing proved to be a greater distraction than burying myself in work.

VALENTINE'S DAY

T HE SHOP WAS busy. Packed even. There was a line out
the door, and we'd never had a line out the door. I'd
already sent the *kids* out for their first set of deliveries,
but at this pace, they'd be working until midnight. It
was the most sales we'd had since the store opened, and it
was only midday.

"Okay, this is insane," Karina said as she wrapped a
dozen roses in paper and placed baby's breath and extra
greenery throughout. "We're going to run out."

I nodded. She was right. We were.

"I know."

It would be the first time that I'd run out of roses on a
holiday before. I'd always had more than I needed, but this
was on another level completely. I hadn't planned for this
kind of traffic because I'd had no idea it would happen.

"Why are we so busy? Not that I'm complaining," I whispered toward Karina as I worked on my own vase bouquet for a waiting customer. "But I don't get why we're way over capacity."

"I have no idea." She shrugged.

Ringing up the order, I smiled at the young guy who had watched me create my masterpiece for him. "Thank you for coming. Hope to see you again."

He smiled back. "Of course you will," he said, and it was a bit of an odd response, but I kept grinning anyway. "The article was great, by the way."

"The article?" I cocked my head and asked, "What article?"

"The one online about shopping local for the holidays," he tossed like I should have known what he was talking about, but I had no idea what he meant. "Search your store name. I'm sure it will pop up," he said as he headed out with a giant vase filled with roses in hand.

I turned toward Karina, meeting her inquisitive expression that I knew matched my own. She pulled out her phone and started typing. She'd find the article before I ever could.

"Can I help you?" I asked the next customer in line. Then, I went to work, grabbing his preordering arrangement.

"Uh, Val?" Karina shoved her phone in my eyeline as I pulled a flower arrangement from the refrigerated display case.

Glancing at the screen, I noticed Jase's name at the top. It was exactly what the guy had said it was. An article about keeping your dollars local for Valentine's Day and how to help small businesses. The name of my flower shop was listed first along with a line telling people to buy from me instead of ordering online, where the picture might not match the reality. Our conversation in Vail flashed through my mind, and I moved her phone out of the way.

"I'll read it later. Send me the link."

"Yep," she said before she started furiously clicking on her phone once more.

I didn't want to think about Jase and what he'd done right now. Plus, I had no idea how to truly feel. Obviously, on one hand, I was grateful for the publicity, especially since it'd contributed to us becoming a local household name. But on the other hand, I still felt betrayed, and no article was going to change the fact that he'd lied to me.

My sadness in regard to Jase had flipped a page, and I was currently in the very angry phase with no clue on when it would end. All I knew was that even with the awesome write-up, I still hated him... even though the day continued in much of the same way.

There was no time for breaks or food. The kids had finished off the last of the deliveries and were currently helping cut ribbon and arrange bouquets in the back room. Right as the clock hit four thirty, I ran out of roses completely, much to the chagrin of the mostly male customers still waiting in line.

My fingers ached, and I had bruises starting to form at the tips as I stepped outside to deliver the news. "I can still make you beautiful arrangements with our other flowers, but I understand if it's not what you want," I announced to everyone, and they fidgeted as they tried to decide what to do.

"Here's a thought." I held up a finger as a couple of men turned their backs to leave. "You can grab some roses from the grocery store and combine them with my arrangement. It's really easy to add them in, but it's up to you."

The men started nodding their heads and returned to the line as I went back inside to create magic with what little we had left until we finally had no more. Blowing out a long, exhausted breath, I flipped the store sign to *Closed* and locked the front door. I wanted to collapse on the tiled floor and sleep for three days, but I made it to the front counter and draped myself over it instead, wishing I had the energy to celebrate today with alcohol.

"Are you going to reach out to him?" Karina asked before letting me know she'd sent the kids home earlier with some extra cash for food and tips.

I didn't even have to ask her who she meant. Of course, she was talking about Jase.

"No," I said without having to think it over.

"Really? Even after what he did for us today?"

"It changes nothing." My tone was very matter-of-fact because it was the truth.

"It changed the hell out of our bottom line. Probably going forward too. We're going to make more money this year than we ever have, all because of his little article."

I lifted my head to glare at my best friend. "Well, it's the least he could have done," I offered sarcastically before pushing up from the counter and sitting on a barstool.

"I think you should read this." She handed me her phone, and I sucked in a breath before begrudgingly taking it and scanning the article.

"It's flattering and well written." It was the most I was willing to give him after all he'd done. Plus, I was still in the angry phase, so there wasn't room for much else.

"There's also one more thing," Karina said, her voice uneven.

I looked at her as unease filtered through my insides. "What is it?"

She disappeared into the back room before reappearing, holding a massive vase filled with red and white roses from our shop. "These are for you." She placed them in front of where I sat, and they were so massive that I couldn't see over them to yell at her.

"We could have used these today, Karina!" There were at least two dozen roses there, and the last thing I would ever do was keep them for myself when they could have gone to someone who needed them.

Sliding the vase to the side so I could see her face, I watched as her eyes squeezed shut before she opened them again.

"Don't kill me. He placed the order last week."

"He who?" I said before the reality sank in. "And you let him?" I was confused to say the least. Karina was the only person who knew every single detail about Jase and me, and she'd still allowed him to buy me flowers? And she'd helped him do it? "You let him buy me flowers? From our store? Why?"

"It was before you saw him at the deli," she countered, as if that made it all okay somehow when it didn't. "Read the card, Val."

"I don't want to read the card."

"Read the damn card." She pulled it from the arrangement and slammed it in front of me. When I made no move to reach for it, she grabbed it and started opening the tiny envelope. "Fine. I'll read it for you."

Glaring at her, I waited to see what wonderful lies Jase had asked her to write and why the hell she was forcing me to go along with whatever this was.

"Turn around," she said, and I wasn't sure if I'd heard her right or not.

"Huh?"

"I said, *turn around.* That's what the card says."

Spinning the barstool, I saw Jase standing outside of the locked front door, looking as gorgeous as I remembered. It wasn't fair. A liar shouldn't be able to be that hot. "Why is he here?"

A knock against the wood redirected my attention.

"You can't come in," I shouted, and Jase looked uncomfortable as he shifted his weight and knocked again, only harder. "I said, go away."

"No," he yelled back, standing his ground.

I spun around to level Karina with my laser-shooting gaze, but she was already walking toward the door, keys in hand.

"Don't you dare," I said. It was a challenge. One I knew I was about to lose as she stuck the key into the hole and turned.

"Thanks," Jase said under his breath as he walked inside.

His hair was disheveled, like he'd been running his fingers through it nonstop, but when his eyes locked on to mine, he let out a relieved breath. I wanted to smack the relief right off his face.

"I'll just, uh," Karina said as she crept away slowly, "be in the back room."

I wanted to murder her for leaving me alone with him.

Why is she being so disloyal?

"Val," he said, his tone almost wary.

"Why are you here?" I growled, not willing to bend so easily. Just because it was hard to look at him and not want him, I refused to be that kind of woman. I never took what wasn't mine. And Jase belonged to someone else. "I want you to leave."

"No." He took another step inside the store, closer to me.

"Leave, Jase," I demanded, hoping my tone sounded stronger than I currently felt. My resolve started to crumble, but I refused to give in.

"Not until you listen to me." He made his way toward the front counter, and I hopped off the barstool and hurried behind the counter, using it as a barrier between us.

"Go. Away."

"Dammit. Listen to me," he yelled.

I'd never seen him lose control before. Then again, I barely knew the guy, so there were lots of sides to him I hadn't seen.

"No," I said, sounding like an unreasonable toddler, but I didn't care. He'd hurt me.

"You're being stubborn." A light laugh escaped him, and it only made me angrier. I watched as his eyes roamed away from me for only a second and landed on the monstrosity next to me. "I see you got my flowers."

Reaching for them, I shoved the heavy glass in his direction, trying not to tip it over in the process. "I don't want them. Don't you have a fiancée you should be buying these for?"

"Yeah, about that," he started to say, and I wondered what lie he'd tell next. "I heard that you saw me in the deli the other day."

I narrowed my eyes at him. "Yep. Can you leave now?"

Another gruff laugh. "It's not what you think," he said, and I wanted to roll my eyes.

"How original," I sniped because wasn't that every guy's go-to line when they got caught doing something wrong? They never admitted anything. It was always deny, deny, deny until it couldn't be denied any longer.

"Look at me," he said, his tone no longer kind or filled with humor.

I shook my head, refusing to listen or do as he asked. Jase Malone wasn't the boss of me, and he could go right to hell.

He reached across the counter between us and almost touched my hand before I pulled it away in the nick of time. That had been close. Skin-on-skin contact might have made me give in to his demands. Locking my jaw, I forced my eyes downward and stared at my feet.

"You asked for it," he warned before hopping onto the counter and grabbing me hard. I struggled, wanting him to stop touching me, but he was so much stronger than I was. "Stop fighting and look at me."

"No," I growled out, swatting at his chest and shoulders. "Let go of me, you liar."

"Jesus, Val. I want you to look at me when I say this, but you're so damn difficult. That was my sister!" he screamed, and my arms fell to my sides as he cupped my chin.

HIS SISTER?

I DIDN'T MOVE.

I didn't breathe.

I still refused to make eye contact.

"That was my sister. The person you saw me with. The one wearing a giant ring. Val, are you listening to me?"

He finally let go of my face, and only then did I allow my eyes to meet his stunning blue ones. They were just as I remembered—all gorgeous and deep.

"Your sister?" I asked as the foggy haze started to lift.

"Yes. My little sister. Her name's Astley."

Oh, how my heart begged me to believe him.

But what if he isn't telling the truth? my brain interjected, all reasonable and annoying even though it was right.

The last thing I wanted to be was stupid, and Jase made me feel that way sometimes—all void of reason and jumping in with both feet.

"How do I know you're not lying?"

He reached in his pocket, pulled out his cell phone, and shoved it into my hands. "Here. Call her."

This is a trick, my head warned.

It's not a trick, my heart pleaded.

The two warred inside me as I held his phone in my hands, wondering what the right thing to do was.

Isn't it enough that he said I could call her to prove his point? my heart asked.

That's just part of the trickery, my head warned.

"I think I will," I said as my stomach twisted into knots. "Call her, I mean. Astley, you said?" I asked as I started pressing buttons on his phone to make her name pop up, and I watched his reaction, carefully measuring it as I poised my finger over the Call button.

He looked a little uneasy, and I had no idea what that meant, but it was better that I knew the whole truth now rather than continue with some sort of charade. I pressed the button, and the phone rang, my mouth suddenly drier than the Sahara Desert.

"Hey, big brother," a female voice said as she snapped what sounded like bubblegum across the line.

"Uh, hello?" I started fumbling. I hadn't thought about

what I was going to say, and now, I was at a loss, sounding like a fool.

"Oh!" she said, her tone overly excited. "Is it you? From Vail? The flower-store girl?"

The smile crept onto my face without warning, and Jase visibly relaxed as he noticed it too. "Yes, it's me. Val."

"Thank God. My brother won't shut up about you. It's so annoying," she said with a laugh, and my heart sprouted hands and started clapping with her words.

"Really?" I tried to sound composed, but my voice cracked a little.

She groaned. "Yes. He told me all about you the second he got home and literally hasn't stopped since. I told him to find you. That even though you said you didn't want to see him, it was only because you were scared. Was I right? Please tell me I was right. I would love to rub that in his face." She talked a mile a minute, but every word replaced the dread in my body and filled it with hope instead.

I swallowed hard, my eyes locked on to Jase. "Pretty much."

"I knew it!" she shouted before laughing. "Are you with him right now? Duh, of course you are. You called me from his phone."

"Yeah. He's right here," I said, my gaze still holding on

to his.

I had to stop myself from throwing my body into his arms and telling him how sorry I was for jumping to conclusions. Jase hadn't been lying to me.

"Oh, hey. I didn't even ask why you were calling in the first place," she said as if she suddenly remembered that I'd called her phone and not the other way around.

My cheeks heated with my embarrassment, and I knew they were turning beet red. "Well, to be honest, I saw you with Jase at a deli last week," I said, and she cut me off.

"Oh my God. Don't they make the best sandwiches in the world? I love that place!" she shouted before sucking in a breath. "Wait. You saw us there? Why didn't you say hi?"

I pursed my lips together before blurting out, "I thought you were his fiancée."

"Ewwww." She dragged out the word for so long that it made me giggle. "Gross. No. Why would you think that?"

"Because he had his arm around you. And you were wearing a ring."

"This whole past week, you thought he had a girlfriend?"

"Fiancée," I corrected because the difference in title clearly mattered.

"And that's why you're calling me right now? To make

sure he's not some lying douche bag?"

"Yeah. Pretty much."

"I don't know everything he told you in Vail, but from what I do know, he told you the truth. My brother's not really a liar. He doesn't have a girlfriend or a fiancée. And I've never seen him as enamored with anyone the way he seems to be with you."

Damn. That was one solid sales pitch. This family seems to be great at them.

"Do you think I'm crazy?" I asked because, now, I wanted her to like me.

"Hell no," she said with a snarky tone. "I'd do the exact same thing. I'm a little psycho when it comes to my man, so I get it." She started laughing hysterically through the phone, and I pulled it away from my ear. "How did you not rip our heads off when you saw us together? I would have lost my ever-loving shit if it were me."

"I was too stunned to do anything but run out of there as fast as I could," I explained.

"You're a better woman than me. I would have created the world's biggest scene and hoped everyone was filming it."

I laughed. "You and my best friend are going to get along really well."

"Can you two do this female-bonding shit some other time?" Jase said, suddenly all up in my space, his warm breath skirting against my skin.

"I, uh, gotta go, Astley."

"See you soon," she singsonged into the phone, and the call ended.

I watched as her smiling picture disappeared from the screen before handing the phone back to Jase.

"Do you believe me now?" he asked.

Karina shouted from the back room, scaring me half to death, "If she doesn't, I do."

"Why are you still here?" I moved away from Jase's commanding presence and headed toward the room, where Karina was sitting on top of the workstation, kicking her feet back and forth. Jase refused to give me space, following right behind.

"I was just waiting for the right moment before I took off," she explained. "And I wanted to show you this."

Karina shoved her phone at me, a text message thread between her and Jase from earlier that morning showing on the screen.

Why is everyone throwing their phones at me today?

KARINA: YOU STILL WANT ME TO GIVE HER THOSE ROSES?

JASE: ABSOLUTELY. WHY? IS THERE A REASON I SHOULDN'T?

KARINA: YOU TELL ME.

JASE: I'M CONFUSED.

KARINA: HEARD YOU'RE ENGAGED, ASSHOLE.

JASE: I'M WHAT???

KARINA: ENGAGED. AND APPARENTLY, STUPID TOO. POOR GIRL.

JASE: I AM NOT ENGAGED. WHAT THE HELL ARE YOU TALKING ABOUT?

KARINA: VAL SAW YOU WITH A GIRL AND A GIANT RING. SHE THINKS YOU LIED TO HER.

JASE: WHEN? WHERE?

KARINA: AT SOME DELI. IT WAS LAST WEEK.

JASE: FUUUUUUCK. THAT WAS MY SISTER.

KARINA: BETTER NOT BE LYING.

JASE: I'M NOT. GIVE HER THE ROSES, PLEASE. PUT TURN AROUND ON THE CARD. I'LL BE WAITING OUTSIDE WHEN YOU CLOSE THE SHOP.

KARINA: YOU OWE ME.

JASE: TILL THE DAY I DIE.

I stopped scrolling when I reached the end of the thread. "Thank you," I said as I handed her back her cell.

"Didn't want you to hate me," she said as she hopped off the workstation and reached for her jacket. "I'm going now. You aren't going to kill him, right?" She gave Jase a look before waiting for my answer.

"No."

"Are you going to *do it* back here? I would. I totally would," she said, and Jase choked out a laugh.

"Go away," I urged, hoping she'd leave without mortifying me any further.

"What? I was just being honest," she said as she headed out the back door, and I locked it behind her.

Jase stared at me, his eyes looking at me like they had when we were in Vail—all predatory and filled with lust. He placed both hands on the table and pushed down on it repeatedly. "Not a bad idea," he said, and I swatted his shoulder.

"Stop," I said because my emotions had just whiplashed back and forth.

I wanted Jase, but I also craved a minute or two to process everything I'd learned. The main cause of the hurt was gone, but the remnants still remained.

He stepped toward me cautiously, his hands reaching for

my arms. "Vail wasn't a fling for me. I thought I'd be okay once I got back here, but I couldn't stop thinking about you. You won't leave my thoughts. Tell me you can't stop thinking about me."

"Of course I can't stop thinking about you," I said, and he inhaled like it was the first breath he'd taken in weeks.

"Thank God."

He leaned forward and claimed my mouth, making sure I knew that no one would ever kiss me the way Jase Malone did. I dived into that kiss with both feet, knowing exactly where it was leading and the road we were heading down.

Kissing Jase meant that we were going all in—together. Vail hadn't been a fling. It had been the start of something deeper, and I'd known that, which was why I'd run, too concerned with how it would look to other people or what they might say.

"Going on that trip was the best thing that's ever happened to me," he said as he broke the kiss, and I swore I had to stop myself from tearing up.

"Me too. I'm sorry I told you I didn't want to see you," I started to explain, but he put a finger to my lips, silencing me.

"No more apologies."

A thought hit me in that moment. "One more," I said,

and he winced like it made him physically uncomfortable. "I never thanked you for the necklace. I loved it. I wore it every day until the deli incident."

"Then, what did you do with it?"

"Put it back in the box. Almost threw it in the trash, but I couldn't bring myself to actually do it," I admitted.

There had been times when I hung it over the trash can in my apartment, willing my fingers to let it go, but they refused. The one time they'd listened to me, I'd practically dived in after it, wiping off lettuce and additional condiments off the box.

"I'm glad you kept it." He smiled. "Do you have plans?"

"Like, right now?" I looked around my empty store, half-wired from his nearness and exhausted from the day.

"Right now. Can I take you out for Valentine's Day? Or do you have other plans?"

"Well"—I blew out a soft breath before running my fingers down the scruff of his jaw—"this guy wrote an article online about my store."

His eyes widened as he leaned back. "Did he now? Should I be threatened?"

"He is pretty hot," I said, playing along. "Looks like the kind of guy who'd start a fight if provoked."

He reared back again. "Really? Do you like that in a

guy? The fighting kind?"

"I mean, if he was fighting for my honor, I might find that extremely sexy."

Closing the space between us, he held me with one strong arm, pressing my body against his, and I felt every hard muscle. "And this writer guy," he said with a wave of his other hand, "he would fight for your honor?"

Shrugging, I gave him a smirk. "I think so. I mean, he wrote a whole article about my store and made me run out of flowers."

Jase started laughing, his whole body shaking as he stepped away. "You ran out of flowers?"

"Yes! And it's all your fault!"

Scratching his head, he nodded. "Sorry, not sorry."

"About that date," I said, redirecting his focus, "you might have to carry me around. I'm dead on my feet."

"Hop on." He knelt, so I could climb on. "Get on my back, or I'll carry you."

"So bossy," I said as I jumped and he handed me a blanket.

HE IS EVERYTHING

I COULDN'T STOP laughing as Jase carried me piggyback-style while we walked down the street. Well, he walked. I was his little Yoda, all wrapped in a blanket and everything.

"Where are we going?" I whispered in his ear, which made him stop moving.

"Don't do that," he warned. "Do you have any idea how turned on I am right now?"

"What?" I practically shouted as I squirmed to get down, but he held on tighter.

"I've been dreaming about you since I got back, Val. And now, your body is pressed against mine. I can feel your tits bouncing around on my back, and it's giving me a hard-on that might scare people passing by."

"Jase!"

"What?" he asked as he finally allowed me to get off his back.

"You sound like Karina." I frowned as I glanced at his pants. "With your dirty mouth and—" I stopped short because *holy shit.*

He hadn't been lying. That thing might poke someone's eye out if they got too close.

I pointed at it, eyes wide.

"Babe," he said.

My jaw dropped with the affectionate nickname. I fucking loved hearing it slip out of his mouth, knowing that it was meant for me.

"Don't point at it." He looked around before adding, "I made reservations for dinner, but can I take you to my place and feast on you instead?"

I pretended to mull over the question like it was the toughest one I'd been asked all day. Tapping a finger against my lips, I released a breath. "Fine. But you'll still have to feed me at some point," I warned because I was starving.

He grabbed my hand hard and tugged me toward the street while his other hand flew into his mouth as he whistled for a cab.

"Damn, someone's motivated," I mumbled under my

breath, but he heard me.

"I don't think I could have made it through dinner without trying to fuck you under the table. Or in the restroom," he said as a cab stopped for us, and we climbed inside. Jase shouted an address, and the driver sped off into the night.

Normally, I would have been more embarrassed by Jase's dirty talk, but I was turned on. Knowing that I made him that crazy was empowering. His hand was on my thigh while the other one was busy, frantically typing out on his phone. I had no idea what he was doing, and to be honest, I couldn't have cared less.

Two hours ago, I'd thought I'd never see Jase Malone again, and now, I was heading back to his place with him. Yesterday, I would have bet money that he was engaged to be married, and today, I knew there was no one he'd rather be with than me. Last week, I would have stopped myself from leaving with him, afraid that I was being rash and acting without thinking. And tonight, I knew that there were no rules when it came to your heart and who it craved—regardless of time and how much had passed between loves.

"We're here," he said, and I smiled at him before peeking outside. He handed the driver some cash and exited, holding out a hand for me to take to help me out of the car.

"Such a gentleman."

"My mama raised me right," he said as we approached his building. It was nicer than mine, had a doorman and everything, which I was a little bit impressed with.

We stepped into the warm air of the lobby and toward the bank of elevators.

Jase spun me in his arms and whispered against me, "I'm spending the rest of my life with you. You know that, don't you?"

I blushed as my body heated with his words. Looking up into his blue eyes, I didn't respond with words, way too nervous to agree, so I kissed him instead. And he called me out on it. Of course he would.

"I'll take your nonanswer as an answer. You think it's too soon. But when you know, you know. At least, that's what they always say."

The elevator dinged, and we got in, my thoughts racing, my heart pounding.

To be honest, I wasn't sure what I truly believed anymore. Yes, it seemed way too soon to talk about things like that, but it also felt oddly right and comforting even though I refused to admit all of that to anyone but myself. At least, not yet.

We stopped on the eleventh floor and walked hand in hand down a long hallway. Jase pulled out a key and unlocked his front door, and we stepped inside the modest apartment. It was bigger than mine but not by much. A typical New York dwelling—small and, what I assumed was most likely, overpriced.

He stopped in the living room–slash–dining room and turned to face me. "I want to devour every inch of your body, Val. You consume me," he said, and I sucked in a breath with his admission. "When you said you didn't want to see me again, you fucking killed me. I couldn't take it. I couldn't breathe. I had to leave," he explained, and I knew that for the moment, he was back in my hotel room in Vail, getting his heart broken all over again.

"I was trying to do the right thing, but I couldn't stop thinking about you. Then, I saw you in the deli," I explained, and he started shaking his head.

"I hate that you thought that I'd deceived you," he said, his eyes wincing like he was in physical pain. "How you must have felt. I would never do that to you."

"I know." I wanted to take away his pain, to move past that part in our story. "I mean, I know that now."

"Do you?" he asked.

I nodded because my gut told me to trust him. "Yes."

"Good, because I'll never lie to you. Even when it hurts, I'll tell you the truth."

I swallowed hard. His tone was so serious. It was like we'd skipped the lighthearted dating phase and taken a sharp turn into committed territory and parked there.

"I won't lie to you either."

"I have to ask you something," he said before there was a knock at the door.

"Expecting company?" I asked.

"Actually …" He opened the door and thanked someone there before reappearing with bags of food. "I promised my girl that I'd feed her."

Breathing in the air, I inhaled long and deep, the smell of Italian food saturating my senses. He really did think of everything.

"I don't care what it is; I want it all now."

He laughed as he pulled container after container out of the bags and set them on the counter. "I wasn't sure what you'd like, so I got a bit of everything."

And he had. There was a pizza, two kinds of pasta, meat and cheese ravioli, three different types of sauce, and a fresh loaf of bread.

My stomach growled as I looked, wanting all of it. "Will you think differently of me if I take some of literally every-thing?" I asked with a cautious grin.

"I'll like you even more than I already do."

"You say that now," I teased. "What happens when I'm so full that I can barely walk?"

"I'll carry you," he said without thinking.

I watched as he pulled out a mini cheesecake in the shape of a heart and put it in the fridge before handing me a plate and taking one for himself.

"Ladies first."

I hadn't been joking when I said I wanted some of everything. I literally put a little bit of each on my plate before moving to the tiny couch that as currently doubling as my table and sitting down.

"This is the perfect end to the perfect day," I said before even taking a bite. "Thank you for everything. And thank you for the write-up."

"You already thanked me," he said, his plate filled with even more food than mine as he sat down next to me.

"I'm not sure I did." I forked a cheese-filled tortellini with pesto sauce into my mouth and moaned as I chewed. "Wait! You said you had something to ask me," I said, suddenly remembering.

He held up a finger until he finished swallowing his bite. "I was going to see if you wanted to come to my parents' for dinner tomorrow night."

I started choking on my food. "What? You want me to

meet your parents already?" I suddenly felt like some sort of high school teenager who didn't know what to do instead of a grown-ass businesswoman who had her shit together and could handle meeting them.

Jase shrugged like it was no big deal. "You're going to meet them eventually. Why wait?"

My stupid heart and brain started warring again inside me. No matter how many times I told my mind to shut the hell up, it refused to listen.

"Val, we're adults. We don't have to wait for you to meet my parents. Or to move in together. Or to get engaged. We can do whatever we want, whenever we want to do it. It's our life, and no one gets to dictate how we live it, except the two of us."

"You and your speeches," I exclaimed, realizing that I'd never said that out loud before. "So, what's tomorrow?"

"Their anniversary. A small gathering. I have to go, obviously, but it would be so much better if you were there with me."

"How many years have they been married?"

"You won't believe me if I tell you."

"Try me." I poked his shoulder.

"Thirty years." He raised his eyebrows, and I instantly started doing the math in my head. "They got married in the fall after graduating high school."

"Wow. Will your sister be there too?" I perked up at the thought.

Astley sounded like fun, and I was looking forward to meeting her in person.

"Unless she wants to die, yes."

"Okay, Mr. Malone, I'll be your plus-one."

He leaned across the couch and kissed me, his breath tasting like garlic and meatballs—and trust me, I didn't mind in the least. "Are you done eating for now? I need to be inside you."

"Well, when you put it that way," I said, immediately dropping the fork in my hand. My body was lifted into the air by a pair of strong arms before my fork had a chance to make contact with the coffee table.

Jase carried me into his bedroom and had his way with me for what felt like hours, my brain short-circuiting with every orgasm. My body was sore, my senses overloaded. But even being completely satiated, I gave in to him when he begged "just one more" for the fourth time.

The man's appetite for me was insatiable.

And I wouldn't have it any other way.

LIFE-CHANGING TRAVEL DEALS

SIX MONTHS LATER

'D ENDED UP going to his parents' anniversary party the next night, and they'd welcomed me with open arms—and hearts. The two of them had been high school sweethearts, who still adored each other to this day. And it showed.

Each one acted as if the other had hung the moon in the sky. It made me realize where Jase had gotten his romantic nature from. Not to mention, the whole "when you know, you know" phrase that he'd repeated to me on more than one occasion. Those exact words had been in his dad's speech to his mom that night.

It'd made me tear up.

Astley, Jase's sister, was a riot in the best possible way. A tiny hurricane with a big mouth, and I'd loved her instantly. She was engaged but hadn't even started planning or thinking about the wedding yet. She claimed she wasn't in a rush to walk down the aisle and wanted to enjoy this stage of their relationship before they got hitched and were pressured for babies nonstop.

Her husband-to-be agreed, but I got the feeling that he would do whatever she asked just to make her happy. I liked them together, but I remembered thinking that if Jase ever proposed to me, I'd probably want to get married the very next day. There was no way I'd be able to sit on my hands and wait it out.

Nothing about our relationship had been slow. We moved with lightning-quick speed, but honestly, it seemed to suit us. We'd talked about moving in together, and the craziest part of all was that none of it felt even remotely crazy. I basically lived at Jase's apartment every night anyway.

I'd been with Moore for three years, and we had been no closer to living together at the end of our relationship than we'd been when we first started dating. It was so interesting whenever I realized the differences between the two men.

When I looked back at Moore and me, it felt like a lifetime ago. Who I was now, with Jase, wasn't who I had been when I was with Moore. I wasn't sure he'd recognize this girl anymore, all full of life and having experiences outside of New York. Not often, but more than I'd ever thought I would.

My mom had mentioned something similar after I brought Jase home to meet her. She loved him, of course. Said that he was *the one*, and she'd never once said that about Moore. Last I'd heard, he was still in London with no plans to come back to the States.

I hoped he was happy.

Who would have thought that a three-day getaway could lead to such a fulfilling love life? Who would have thought that I'd meet my soul mate during a price-saving-induced trip?

Love worked in funny ways.

Time had her hands in everything.

If Moore hadn't broken up with me, I wouldn't have tried to prove something to myself and booked that last-minute trip. Vail never would have happened for me. Not in a million years.

And if Jase's coworker hadn't broken his leg before the trip, he never would have been there either.

Sometimes, I thought fate loved playing with us mere mortals.

But I wasn't complaining. Because meeting Jase was the very best thing that had ever happened to me. I'd thought I knew what love was, but I realized that whatever I'd had with Moore wasn't this. It had been a type of love, but it hadn't been the kind that lasted. It hadn't been what dreams were made of or what made couples stay married and get through the hard stuff.

I saw that now.

Had Moore and I stayed together, we would have burned out in a blaze eventually, destroying everything and everyone around us.

"Ahem," Karina cleared her throat, pulling me out of my internal monologue.

"Was I talking out loud again?" I asked because, apparently, I'd been doing that lately. Having all of these deep conversations with myself but not keeping all of the words inside.

"No, but you had 'the face,' " she said, using air quotes around the words. Karina had dubbed me having "the face" whenever I got lost in thought or wasn't really present in the moment.

"I ordered an extra five dozen reds for the upcoming weekend," she said, showing me a notepad, and my eyes widened.

"We sold out again?" I asked because I'd thought we finally had our system figured out to where we wouldn't run out of anything without warning.

Jase's Valentine's Day article had given us a new steady influx of customers, but when the magazine had given him the okay to write a printed article, well, that had sent business through the proverbial roof. We had run out of roses … *again*. Which only made me mad … *at myself*.

"It's all your boyfriend's fault," she said.

I huffed out a laugh. "I know. What a jerk."

"The biggest." She tapped her pen on top of the notepad. "You sure he doesn't have a brother or a cousin? I could use a good jerk in my life," she asked for, like, the hundredth time.

"I wish he did," I said, meaning it. "You know I'd set you up in a heartbeat."

The best part about Jase was that he was exactly the kind of man he had presented himself to be when we first met.

His words were true.

His actions even truer.

"Well, he doesn't. And it's kind of rude, just so you both know." She propped out her hip and snarled before giggling. "Are you all packed?"

I nodded. "My bag is in the back."

Jase had told me to pack for two days. He'd said we were going away, but he wouldn't tell me where we were headed. A year ago, I would have scoffed and fought against leaving the store, insisting that there was nowhere else in the world I needed to be, except for behind that counter. But Jase made adventuring appealing. And I couldn't say no to him anyway.

"You still have no idea where you're going?" Karina asked with a smirk that let me know that she knew.

I swatted her shoulder. "Oh my gosh, you know!"

"Of course I know." She mimicked my tone. "He can't say he wants to take you away without giving me all the details."

"I hate that you know," I lied. I really didn't care that Karina knew what Jase was up to before I did. It was only a matter of time before I saw our location anyway.

"Your knight in shining armor has arrived." Karina wagged her eyebrows and nodded toward the front door.

Jase's muscular frame was heading up the pathway, and just seeing him put a smile on my face. The bell on the door jingled as he pulled it open.

"Hey, beautiful." He swept me into his arms and planted a kiss on my lips. "We gotta go."

"Let me grab my bag," I said before disappearing into

the back.

I came back out to the sound of Jase harassing Karina. "You told her, didn't you?"

She stomped a foot against the floor. "Well, I never!"

"She didn't," I interjected, and Jase laughed.

"I know. She's the best secret-keeper ever." He pulled her into a hug as she squirmed and pretended to hate it, but I knew better. My best friend loved the attention.

"Go away. See you in a couple days." She started pushing Jase's body away and toward the door. "Take your dumb boyfriend, Val," she directed, still shoving as I exited the store without worrying or complaint.

We headed from the shop to the airport. The secret destination could only be held on to until we walked up to security, and Jase handed me my boarding pass.

Vail.

"We're going to Vail?" I looked at him with wide eyes.

We'd talked about going back when it wasn't filled with snow, just so we could experience it in a different season, but I hadn't expected it so soon.

"Summer in Vail, babe," was all he said in response before tugging me against his side and holding me tight.

"Where are we staying?" I asked.

He shook his head. "No questions. Just let go and let me

surprise you."

I pouted. "But I'm already surprised."

WE ARRIVED IN Vail right before the sun was starting to set. Stepping out of the car and into the warm air, I breathed in deep, appreciative that there wasn't a drop of humidity to be found. The entire mountain town was filled with a golden glow that looked like it was straight out of an animated fairy movie. I'd always thought this place was magical in the winter, but summer seemed to hold the same appeal.

Maybe it was just that Vail bore the magic and not the time of year.

"I forgot how pretty it was here," I said as I looked around, taking in all the lush greens that had been covered in white on our last visit. "It looks so different."

Jase nodded in agreement, his camera snapping pictures before he could stop himself. "It's so colorful. The flowers," he said before stopping, clearly getting lost in the gorgeous decor of the main street.

Multicolored flowers were draped over balconies and

hung from oversize pots attached to the light poles. There were planters in front of every store and so many trees lining the street.

I pointed at the snow-capped mountain in the distance. "There's still snow."

"I think there always is. We're pretty high up, elevation-wise," he said.

My little Mr. Know-It-All.

As we both stared at our surroundings, he squeezed me tight and whispered in my ear, "I'm spending the rest of my life with you. You know that, right?"

"So you keep saying," I countered before pulling out of his embrace and doing what I always did whenever he said that—I flashed him the empty ring finger on my left hand. Which only made him laugh.

"Come on. Let's go get checked in."

Jase wrapped his arm around my waist, and we walked into the same hotel where we'd first met. He told me to stay put while he went and checked us in, and I waited with the luggage for him to return with our keys.

"Let's go." He grabbed both of our bags and headed toward the elevator.

It was surreal, being in this place again with him. I wondered if any of the same staff still worked here and if they'd remember us or not. When the elevator halted at the third floor, I didn't think anything of it. But as Jase walked down the familiar hallway and stopped in front of our room, I gave him a funny look.

"We have the same room?" I asked, noticing that it was the one I'd stayed in when I came here. The very room where we'd first had sex … where Jase had asked to see me again and I'd told him no.

"I asked for it," he said all nonchalant and sexy before pressing the key to the pad and pushing the door open for me.

What greeted me was vastly different than the first time I'd stayed here. There were vases upon vases filled with long-stemmed red and white roses. Red rose petals formed a small pathway, highlighted by votive candles on each side, that led to the bed, where more rose petals waited. White balloons covered the entire ceiling in places, and my eyes started watering before my mind could process what was going on.

I turned around to face Jase, but he wasn't there. My eyes went wild before looking down. He was on the ground. On one knee specifically, holding a ring in his massive hand.

"I knew you were different from other girls the first day

we met. I'd never been more comfortable with anyone in my life until you. You inspire me. You challenge me. You are my partner in every way, and I never want to lose any part of that. Tell me you'll be mine forever. Marry me, Val. Say yes to going through the ups, the downs, and all the in-betweens."

Tears streamed down my cheeks, and as I wiped them away, I answered through what I only hoped was a smile, "Yes. Yes. Of course, I'll marry you. There's no one else I'd rather spend forever with than you, Jase Malone."

He slipped the ring on my finger, and it wasn't until then that I noticed the little bears from Vail on each end, delicately woven into the design, holding a massive diamond between their little noses. This man was perfect, and I knew our life together would be the same, no matter what it threw at us.

All because I'd taken a chance and done something completely out of my comfort zone. Not only had I shown myself that there was more to life than my flower shop, but I'd also gotten me a fiancé! I won!

THE END

Thank You

Thank you so much for reading the second book in the Fun for the Holiday's collection! I hope you enjoyed reading this one as much as I did. I love Lily & Jase so much! I came up with the idea for my Fun for the Holiday's Collection to give you lighthearted, happy reads that you could get lost in. I know that the world has been crazy lately, hopefully this helped you escape… if only for a little while. <3

About the Author

Jenn Sterling is a Southern California native who loves writing stories from the heart. Every story she tells has pieces of her truth in it as well as her life experience. She has her bachelor's degree in radio/TV/film and has worked in the entertainment industry the majority of her life.

Jenn loves hearing from her readers and can be found online at:

Blog & Website:

www.j-sterling.com

Twitter:

www.twitter.com/AuthorJSterling

Facebook:

www.facebook.com/AuthorJSterling

Instagram:

@AuthorJSterling